BLACK'S BEACH SHUFFLE

BLACK'S BEACH SHUFFLE

A Novel

Corey Lynn Fayman

iUniverse, Inc.

New York Lincoln Shanghai

Black's Beach Shuffle

iUniverse books may be ordered through booksellers or by contacting:

iUniverse
2021 Pine Lake Road, Suite 100
Lincoln, NE 68512
www.iuniverse.com
1-800-Authors (1-800-288-4677)

This is a work of fiction. All of the characters, names, incidents, organizations, and dialogue in this novel are either the products of the author's imagination or are used fictitiously.

ISBN-13: 978-0-595-40267-0 (pbk)
ISBN-13: 978-0-595-84643-6 (ebk)
ISBN-10: 0-595-40267-4 (pbk)
ISBN-10: 0-595-84643-2 (ebk)

Printed in the United States of America

CHAPTER 1

▼

THE MANSION

It was two-thirty on a Sunday morning in June. Rolly Waters parked his old Volvo wagon outside the gates of a mansion, which sat on the cliffs overlooking the Pacific Ocean just north of La Jolla. It was Rolly's second visit to the house that evening. If he'd been more diligent about packing his instruments after the first visit, he wouldn't have needed to make the second. Somewhere on the other side of the eight-foot high stucco wall that surrounded the house was his 1965 Gibson ES-335 Thinline electric guitar. He wouldn't have been able to sleep knowing it was lying there, all alone, unprotected.

Any decent guitar player develops a special attachment to certain instruments that come along in his life, and Rolly was madly in love with the cherry red Gibson. It was a symbol of promises he'd made to himself, of changes he'd made in his life. It was also worth four thousand dollars. His car was only worth two thousand, at most. The value of the guitar was still increasing. It was the only thing he owned that could be called an investment.

He opened the door, climbed out of the car, and walked across the street. Except for the light shining from the button on the intercom at the gate, the house looked completely dark. Rolly paused for a moment, considered his choices, hoping he wouldn't have to wake anyone. He hated bothering people and, when he was sober, was as considerate in his behavior as anyone could expect from a thirty-nine-year-old rock musician. He hadn't had a drink in four years, ten months, and five days now. His level of solicitousness had risen appreciably in that time. Still, his guitar might be lying on the lawn behind that wall, soaking up dew from the grass, salt mist from the ocean. He needed to overcome his reticence in order to retrieve it before any irreparable damage was done.

He pushed the intercom button, waited, pushed it again. There was no response from the house. If anyone was inside, they were fast asleep, a sleep deepened no doubt by the steady flow of champagne that had been part of the evening's festivities. He pushed the button again. There was still no response.

It was Moogus, the band's drummer, who'd insisted everything had been packed. Moogus was a man possessed of infinite jests and a walloping backbeat, but he was not the kind of man you could depend on. Moogus had been in such a hurry to leave that Rolly had foregone his usual last sweep of the scene. The Volvo was packed full of gear—Moogus' drum cases, Rolly's amplifier, guitars, and kit bag, so it wasn't until they stopped at Moogus' house to unload that Rolly realized the ES-335 was missing.

Rolly searched along the wall that fronted the street. If his calculations were correct, the bandstand had been set up against the other side of the wall about thirty feet to his left. It stood flush against the inside wall, facing the pool and a large concrete patio. The guitar was sure to be somewhere close to the bandstand. If he could get over the wall, he'd be in and out in less than a minute. He walked to his left, along the wall, stepping between the ice plant and a row of small dirt mounds supporting miniature lime trees. He stopped at a spot where he figured the bandstand would be, looked up at the top of the wall. He needed to jump to get his arms over the wall, then try to hang on and drag himself over. He took one step back, looked up, took two more steps back. He balanced himself, ran forward and leapt towards the wall.

Even in his youth, Rolly had never been much of an athlete, and the twenty-five pounds he had put on over the years had not improved his abilities any. He hit the wall stomach first, fell back to the ground. Still, the leap had come close enough that he held out some hope for success. He tried it again, got one arm over the wall, but failed to hold on. After a false start on the third try, he made it on the fourth, throwing both arms across the top of the wall just enough to hang on. He pulled himself up, slid across on his belly, dropped down to the wet grass. A dense silhouette of wooden risers, the bandstand, stood about ten feet off to his left. He walked over to it, searched around the perimeter and under the risers. The guitar wasn't there. The rescue was going to take slightly longer than he had hoped.

He looked towards the patio and the house. The house was shaped like a T laid out flat on the ground. A two-story section formed the top of the T and ran parallel to the edge of the cliffs. It had many tall windows, providing vistas from every room. The stem of the T was a more functional one-story section that divided the patio and pool from the parking lot. A covered walkway provided access between the two areas. If one of the other band members, Gordon or Bruce, had picked up Rolly's guitar case, he would have crossed the lawn to the edge of the patio towards the parking area where they had packed their cars after the gig. It seemed like the place to try next.

Rolly crept across the lawn, stopped at the entrance to the covered walkway, and waited for his eyes to adjust to the darkness inside. He began to make out shapes—a couple of large potted plants, a bicycle, the door to the garage—but there was nothing that resembled the long, flat shape of his guitar case. He felt nervous. A little bubble of gas floated up in his stomach.

He turned back around, scanned the patio. The large round folding tables that had been loaded with towers of jumbo shrimp, trays of sushi, and champagne bottles packed in ice were now empty, reduced to their low-grade wood surfaces and dented metal edges. Bits of red paper tablecloths clung to the spots where they'd been stapled down to keep them from blowing away. On one of the tables stood a couple of champagne flutes the caterers had missed. The party supply company would arrive after sunrise to pick up the tables and chairs, haul them away in their big trucks. Rolly had to find his guitar before they arrived. You never knew what kind of finders/keepers rules the guys who worked the clean-up detail might live by.

He began a methodical walk through the tables, looking under each one, forcing himself to be disciplined. Moogus had been standing out here at the end of the evening, chatting it up with a slinky young woman in a black strapless dress. Moogus' mind worked even less well in the presence of an attractive female.

He spotted the guitar case. It was under one of the tables on the patio, as if someone had shoved it there. He knelt down beside it, flipped the latches and opened the case. The ES-335 was there, safe and snug in the velvet interior lining of its protector. He slapped the cover back down, clicked the latches in place, and grabbed the handle. Everything was right again in his world.

As he turned towards the pool, he saw something he hadn't noticed before, a black shape floating in the water. A stone dropped in Rolly's stomach, sending out ripples. The light from the lamp at the end of the pool surrounded a naked body, creating a silhouette, and the clumps of long black hair that floated around its head made a halo through which bright beams shone, as if the person were departing to meet an alien spaceship, or riding a watery blue light to heaven. Whoever had once inhabited the body was gone now from the earth.

CHAPTER 2

▼

A QUANDARY

The body was skinny, delicate, the figure a little bit girlish. It was hard to tell for sure, but Rolly guessed it was a young man, in his mid-twenties at most. Regardless of age, he was dead; there was no doubt about that. Which left the question of what to do next. Rolly turned, searched for signs of life in the large picture windows that stared down at him. They were silent and dark. An empty balcony hung over the far end of the pool like an elegant, shadowy gallows. Other than the body in the pool and Rolly standing beside it, there was no sign of a human being anywhere. No one had answered his earlier ring at the gate. But it was possible someone was watching him from inside the house even now, someone who might be calling the police. It was an expensive house in an expensive neighborhood. He might have set off some kind of silent alarm without even knowing he'd done it. The security service would have responded by now, sent in a call to the cops.

Rolly looked back at the body and again at the house. Before he could stop himself, he started to run. It was the kind of decision the rational side of his mind had no say in. His feet wouldn't listen to what his mind was trying to say, just like his mouth wouldn't listen to what his mind tried to tell him whenever he used to start drinking. He crossed the lawn at full speed and jumped onto the bandstand, hauling the guitar case with him. Standing on top of the risers, it would be easy to climb over the wall. He placed the case on top of the wall, shoved it over.

He pulled himself to the top of the wall, felt it scrape against his belly. He cursed his expanding middle-aged gut and slid over the edge, plopped down on the ice plant next to his guitar case. He picked up the case, scurried back to his car, and opened the door. He set the case on the passenger seat, sat down beside it, and strapped it in with the seatbelt. The man in the pool had probably been drunk. There hadn't been any blood or signs of a fight that Rolly could see. Just some poor guy who had put away too much champagne and beer, maybe something stronger, then drowned in the pool when no one was watching. Rolly hadn't seen many dead bodies in his life. Two, really, counting tonight. He looked at his watch. It was late.

He flipped on the headlights, turned the key in the ignition. He shifted the gears into drive and pressed on the gas. The engine sputtered and died. Rolly cursed. He turned the headlights off, made a silent promise to himself that if the car started this time, he'd take it to Randy first thing Monday morning. He waited ten seconds, turned the key, and pressed on the gas. The engine sputtered, but it didn't die. He spun a u-turn in the street and headed back out towards Torrey Pines Road and the relative anonymity of a more traveled thoroughfare. He made himself focus on driving, discarding all other thoughts like a man who knew he'd had one too many. He prayed to God he could sneak his way home without seeing a squad car behind him. He took a deep conscious breath, full of effort, then another, trying to slow down the ska-rhythm beat of the blood in his eardrums.

He drove out the winding two-lane road, past the looming shapes of gigantic estates, parked like public announcements for the relentlessly rich, the outer walls wrapped in gnarled, sticky thickets of ivy or bougainvillea. As he slowed to negotiate a sharp left turn, a bright blast of headlights hit him full in the face. Rolly let out a nervous yelp and wrenched the steering wheel to his right. An old Coupe DeVille flew past, inches away from scraping his door. Its headlights whipped through the cabin of the Volvo like a Vari-Lite at a stadium show, then were gone. He turned his head and looked back as the Cadillac's taillights swung around the corner and disappeared. The Volvo bumped against something, came to a stop. Rolly waited, catching his breath. He glanced into the rearview mirror, half expecting to see the Cadillac return. It didn't.

He needed to get going. If a rent-a-cop nitwit or one of S.D.P.D.'s beat boys ran into him before he got out to Torrey Pines Road, they'd pull him over for sure. There would be all sorts of questions about what Rolly was doing in the area at this time of the morning, whether he knew anyone in the neighborhood who could vouch for him. If a rent-a-cop nabbed him, he'd make Rolly wait until the real cops showed up. Then the Finest from America's Finest City would take over, make Rolly squirm for a couple of hours just to prove they'd done their due diligence. They'd ask him the same questions over and over to see if they could catch him saying something two different ways. Rolly had two strikes against him in any beat cop's book. First of all, he was a musician. The guitar and the amplifier would give that one away. Cops hated musicians, especially at two-thirty in the morning.

But it was the identification card Rolly carried in his wallet that would make the cops really antsy—the one with the seal from the state of California that listed his regular profession, his day job. For in the idle hours of the last five years, Rolly had made himself into something other than a musician. He'd worked hard. He'd put in the hours. He'd taken the test and been fully certified as a licensed private investigator.

He was a part-timer, really, like two thousand other guys in town, mostly retired FBI or law enforcement, perhaps ex-Marines, who needed a little cash and something to do because forty-five years old was too young to really retire. But those guys knew how to talk to policemen, had friends who were cops, were part of the club. Rolly got nervous, sloppy, and stupid around anyone in a uniform. He didn't know why. It could have been all those years of late nights, watching his back as he tried to get around in the early hours of the morning, bombed out of his mind. Or maybe it went back to his father, the Navy career man, hiding behind his immaculate white suit and command-level duty while his family had come crashing down all around him.

Rolly returned from his thoughts, brought his eyes back to the Volvo's front windshield. The front fender rested against a large boulder. There was one standing on each side of the road at the entry to The Farms, like net worth boundary markers. They were imported, carved out of granite that had been ripped from the side of an Italian mountain, dropped down here to make suitably weighty and serious sentinels. The cliffs above Black's Beach weren't made out of rocks as solid as these. The cliffs above Black's were made out of sand, hundreds of feet of it, compressed over millions of years. It was fragile, impermanent, slowly giving itself back to the ocean, breaking off in small chunks every day, every month, every year, dropping its leavings down on the beach, sometimes taking some poor tourist or pool cabana down with it.

Rolly put the car into reverse, backed it up a couple of yards and pulled onto the pavement. As he turned onto Torrey Pines Road, he breathed a sigh of relief, felt the knot in his stomach ease up just a little. Leaving the scene had been stupid. But he wasn't going back now. No one had answered his ring at the gate. No one had seen him. His moment of weakness and panic was his own private baggage to carry.

He pulled the car onto Highway 5, south. The baggage started to weigh on his mind. He'd seen a dead man. Someone needed to be told. The party-supply crew would arrive after sunrise, but that left at least three or four hours to go. He'd be at the Pacific Beach off-ramp in less than five minutes. There was sure to be a phone booth at the gas station there, off Garnet. He'd stop and make an anonymous 911 phone call. That was the safest and smartest thing he could do. If anyone ever did make him, he could point the authorities back to his call, use it in defense of his well meant, if somewhat suspicious decision to leave.

He stopped at the gas station, pulled out the photocopied map he'd been given. The letters "BFH," which he assumed were someone's initials, were printed in ornate text on the upper left corner of the paper, next to a roughly sketched map and printed directions to the house. He got out of his car, walked to the phone booth. He dialed the three numbers, reported a dead body in a swimming pool at 1186 Starlight Drive. The operator asked him his name, tried to get more information per their standard procedure. But Rolly stayed with the minimum facts he thought were necessary, then hung up the phone and went back to his car.

He pulled onto Interstate 5, headed south towards downtown San Diego. The traffic was light this time of the morning. He ran through the events of last night in his mind, reviewing the scenes and conversations he could remember, trying to place the dead man among the sea of faces that had passed him the previous evening.

CHAPTER 3

▼

PRE-SHOW JITTERS

It had been a corporate party, given by a company called Eyebitz.com, a local start-up that was making waves, at least according to the *Union-Tribune*'s business section, which Rolly occasionally read. Rolly didn't know much about the Internet or what the company did, but he did have a couple of musician friends who had gone to work at another Internet company in town, MP3.com. Kevin and Rick claimed to be sitting pretty, talking about all the money they were going to make when they went public, whatever that meant. It was one of those mysteries of the financial world that Rolly didn't quite understand, like record company royalty payments. As Rolly saw it, you never really made money unless you were standing at the top of the ant hill. All the worker ants at the bottom would keep on working, thinking they were getting somewhere until the day they got a pink slip because the guy in charge needed a new house in Aspen.

But the Eyebitz.com gig would pay well, especially for a couple hours of actual playing time, which is all that these things ever turned out to be. A company party was sure to include at least one long-winded speech, several employee appreciations and general rah-rah. There was always disorder and confusion over how long and what hours the band was to perform. It wasn't like working down at Patrick's on a Saturday night, with Harry hunting you down and screaming at you if the band stayed on break for more than fifteen minutes.

It was Fender who had set up the gig for the band—Fender "Dodge" Simmons, whom Rolly had known since junior high school. Fender had earned his nickname on the second day of ninth grade when he'd failed to notice he was part of a suddenly improvised game of dodge ball, one in which anyone insignificant and unprotected could suddenly and unknowingly be appointed dodgee by the ruling thugs of the asphalt play yard. Fender was tall, skinny, with a slightly drooped face like a basset hound. He was an okay guy by Rolly, who had always preferred the wallflowers and dweebs to the in-crowd social climbers and power players. Rolly had been an outsider himself, but one who had managed to carry the vague scent of cool by way of his musical skills, pulling in pretty girls and the jocks that followed them with a force they couldn't understand, but couldn't dismiss.

The party started at eight. The band arrived at six-thirty. They set up the equipment and ran a quick sound check. Fender stopped by to show them the room where they could change clothes and stash their belongings. The room was empty, except for a closet, three folding chairs, and an aging white carpet. All of the rooms they passed in the long hallway were empty. Fender explained that the house's lone occupant lived at the other end of the hall, on the second floor, in the room with the balcony overlooking the pool. Rolly thought to himself that it would take him a lifetime to fill up the rooms in the house. If you were living alone, you could just start on a new room every year, trash the one you had been using, lock it up and just forget about it. After all, you still had fifteen rooms or so to go.

After the band members had changed and hung up their clothes, Bruce and Gordon headed off to find an out-of-the-way corner of the house where they could smoke a joint without being noticed. Moogus followed Fender back to the patio by the pool to check out the food and the beverage situation. He was probably checking out the female situation, as well. Rolly wanted to avoid the bar, so he walked out to the front deck, which overlooked a large yard that ran to a short stone wall and a dusty cliff top with the ocean 300 feet below. They were on top of the cliffs above Black's Beach, known to locals and tourists alike for its outstanding waves and optional swimwear. To the south, Rolly could see La Jolla Cove and the village. A light breeze blew through his hair as moist ocean air rose up and met the dry desert wind, creating a temporary stalemate in their endless battle for the coastal atmosphere. A thick bank of fog lay a mile offshore.

"Nice gig," said Moogus, walking out onto the deck towards Rolly. "There's a lot of serious talent here."

Talent was Moogus' word for attractive young women. Moogus was pushing forty-eight and making maybe twenty-five thousand a year full-time drumming, but he remained convinced that "the talent" was always waiting and ready for a man of his unfettered masculine skills. Rolly had never known a drummer who wasn't continually horny and on the make, or at least talked like he was.

"Hey, Rolly." It was Fender, following close behind, carrying that slightly off-center gaze he had where he didn't quite look at you.

"Hey, Fender."

"You got a minute? I'd like to introduce you to some of the folks here. There're important people you should get to know."

Rolly hated meeting important people he should get to know. It made him nervous. He never knew what to say around people with money and power. It looked like these people had plenty. But he needed to be polite to his patrons. It was good business. He stepped off the deck and followed Fender around the garden path to the pool area. On the patio underneath the balcony next to the pool, a small group of sycophants had gathered around a short, skinny man with blond hair. He looked about fourteen years old to Rolly, wiry, nervous. The man moved his hands a lot as he talked, waving a dark bottle of micro-brewed beer in the air. The group standing with him looked spellbound, holding their bottles of beer or glasses of champagne at their sides, as if afraid raising the drinks to their lips suggested a lack of respect. Fender nosed his way in.

"Ricky, I wanted you to meet Rolly Waters. He's a good friend of mine and he's with the band that's going to be playing tonight. Rolly, this is Ricky Rogers, the man with the vision."

Ricky Rogers interrupted his talking to grab Rolly's hand and shake it enthusiastically. He had a big blonde freckled head and bright blue eyes that stared straight into yours, then into the back of your head, through your skull, and out beyond to some horizon that only he could see. Rolly wondered if that was why Fender referred to Ricky as "the man with the vision."

"Glad to meet you, Rolly. Fender tells me you're quite a musician. That's great. We're glad you could be here, be a part of our family."

Rolly wasn't sure he wanted to be a part of any more families. He had a hard enough time with his own. He'd read about Ricky in the paper, a beach rat from Orange County who'd made a million dollars in the self-empowerment seminar market, selling recordings of his gung-ho speeches set to the sound of the surf in the background. Now he was running this Internet company. People said he was going to make a hundred times more. The immediate presence of money and power along with the beer Ricky was waving around made Rolly wish he had a drink. But that would only make him feel worse. It always had. How much was this guy going to be worth, a hundred million billion or something?

"Th-thanks." Rolly stuttered.

"Hey, that's great. We're glad to have you playing for us." Ricky's voice was bright, a little on the high-pitched side. He was a very "up" personality type.

Fender jumped in. "Yeah, Ricky, I've known Rolly since high school. We always knew he was going to be a great musician. He'll get this party rocking!" Fender made it sound as if he had played a critical role in the development of Rolly's musical skills. Fender had been a bit of a groupie in the old days, dropping by uninvited to their rehearsals, sneaking backstage, acting like he was part of the band. But that was just Fender's way. He needed a little self-stroking, especially in front of "important" people, the boss or whoever it was. He was okay when you talked to him all on his own.

The boss was already moving away from them, reaching out a hand to yet another incoming partygoer who had honed in on him like a stock-option-seeking scud missile. Ricky was a man in constant motion.

"Yeah, that's great," he said as he left. Ricky seemed to be fond of the word "great." Maybe everything was great when you were going to be worth as much as Ricky.

Fender's smile dropped away for a second as Ricky moved on, then rebounded again as he turned back to Rolly.

"Ricky's a great guy."

"So I can see," Rolly said. "What does he do, exactly?"

"He's the man with the plan, the visionary. He gets it."

"Gets what?"

"This whole Internet thing, the new economy. He knows how to stay on top of the wave, make opportunities happen."

Rolly had enough troubles with the old economy. He'd never be able to handle a new one. Well, maybe Fender was ready for it. He half sounded like he knew what he was talking about.

"You're in pretty tight with these guys, huh, Fender?"

"Yeah, Rolly. I really think this is going to be it."

Rolly had given up on whatever "it" was a long time ago, but Fender was still out there chasing "it" down. Rolly was fine with his life as it was now, writing songs and playing guitar, chasing down deadbeat dads and teenage runaways. It wasn't a bad life. It was *his*, at least. Every day now that he wasn't drinking was a success. Somebody else making money was not going to make him jealous, even if it was Fender, who was a nice enough guy, but couldn't put more than three chords together without screwing them up.

They walked back to the front deck, overlooking the cliffs. Moogus was gone, but someone much more attractive had taken his place. She was staring out at the view, a cigarette dangling in one hand by the side of her short leather skirt, a glass of champagne in the other. She had on black stockings and suede, high-heeled boots that came up just past the top of her ankles.

"Hey, Alesis," Fender said.

"Hey, Fender," she said, glancing at both of them before she returned to the view, taking a slow drag on her cigarette. It was a tired voice, whisky deep, with a little bit of Southern slowness to it. She had short black hair, cut in a pageboy with a slash of blonde frosting through the bangs.

"Have you seen King?" Fender asked.

"I don't keep track of him when I'm not at the office."

She was tired, perhaps permanently so. And maybe a little pissed off.

"Just wondering," said Fender. "I wanted Rolly to meet him. Maybe he's in the living room. Rolly, you should meet King, too."

"I think I'll just stay out here for awhile, if that's okay," Rolly replied. There were too many people and too many kinds of liquor back in the house. It made him nervous to be around either one. Besides, there was a dangerous looking woman out here, all by herself. He hadn't sworn off of everything that was bad for him. Not yet.

CHAPTER 4

▼

A POSSIBLE MATCH

Rolly smiled at Alesis. He still had a smile that made an impression. It was a friendly thing that sometimes helped women forgive him for being a man. Alesis smiled back.

"Um, yeah, okay," said Fender, glancing back and forth from Rolly to Alesis, "I'll catch you later."

Fender walked back to the house. Rolly turned and stood next to Alesis, took a look at the side of her face, a quick glance down her blouse. She was older than he'd originally thought, but she still had a lot going for her. Not as much as she used to, but plenty enough. He noticed little lines at the edges of her eyes.

Alesis continued to stare out at the ocean, as if the long lost ship she was looking for might suddenly appear on the horizon.

"Ever been to Japan?" she asked, not really expecting an answer. He decided to give her one, anyway.

"Yeah, once. On a tour."

"What kind of tour?"

"I was in a band. We did a tour there."

She turned her head to look at Rolly.

"You were in a band?"

"Still am. We're playing tonight."

"Oh, yeah? I used to be in a band."

Telling people you were in the band always brought something personal back, memories of one shining youthful moment or confessions of non-talent, failed piano lessons. The confessors were easy to handle. It was the folks who'd had a little bit of success you had to step around like landmines.

"What kind of band?" Rolly asked.

"It was an all-girl band, kind of like the Go-Gos. Only more ... adult. We played in Japan one time."

He wasn't sure what the "adult" comment meant. But before he could think of anything else to say, they were interrupted.

"Alesis!" someone shouted from off to their right. Rolly turned. A man, middle-aged, glared out from the sliding glass door.

"I'm right here," said Alesis, without turning around.

"I can't find my glasses."

"Did you check on top of your head?"

The man put his hand up to his bald pate, where a pair of glasses indeed rested.

"Oh, yes. There they are." He pulled the glasses down over his eyes, inspected his fingernails for a moment, then looked back up.

"I can't find my cell phone, either."

Alesis sighed and rolled her eyes. "Okay, I'm coming." She turned towards Rolly, dropped her cigarette on the deck, stamped it out with her boot.

"Just a word of advice. Never go to work for your ex-boyfriend. It's worse than being married."

She smiled again, for real or just out of habit, then turned and walked slowly away. Rolly watched her depart, felt a warm glow run through his body. She knew how to make an exit. It was the kind of departure that would convince men they should spend a lot of money to make sure she came back.

Rolly returned to the view. Down below him, a skinny young man with a black ponytail played the drunken daredevil, balancing along the edge of the cliff for three young women who were dressed for encouragement in tight summer dresses. The women stood in a safe spot behind the wall watching the young man approach the edge of the cliff. He let out little screams and then laughed as the girls reached out to pull him back towards safety. It was the kind of thing Rolly might have tried when he was younger, tempting fate for dramatic effect, craving attention, unaware of the invisible nearness that death always has. He knew now that invisible things can make themselves seen in an instant. It made him nervous watching the young man's balancing act. He turned back to the house.

*   *   *   *

Rolly's thoughts returned to the present, heading south on Interstate 5 towards downtown. He was about to miss the exit to Hillcrest, and home. He took a quick look back, ripped the car across two lanes of traffic, made the exit with a hundred feet to spare.

What had really returned him from his thoughts was the realization that the young man he'd seen dancing along the edge of the cliff might have been the same man he'd seen floating in the pool, the one who had flirted with death earlier that evening. The man in the pool had the same long hair as the man on the cliffs. But Rolly hadn't looked closely at either one. There were several men at the party with long hair.

He headed up Washington, across First, saw the lights of the La Posta Taco Shop up ahead. His stomach felt empty with hunger, or from stress, probably both. He pulled up to the drive-in menu, ordered a *carne asada* burrito and a *Horchata* to drink. There was a small group of gothic-styled teenagers gathered around the front order window, black in their clothes, pale in their makeup. He wondered how many had parents who were drunk or divorced or had hit them, if any were runaways he might be asked to track down. He watched the young Mexican woman inside the bright fluorescent kitchen dip a ladle into a pot of greasy, spiced meat, spread it out on a flour tortilla, then expertly fold it into a little package for filling the stomach of one of the kids who waited outside. Rolly pulled up to the window, asked for a couple of extra packets of hot sauce and picked up his order. He looked forward to feeding his own little hunger, then falling asleep. He glanced at the open door of the liquor store across the street, thought about how his meal might taste with a beer, decided not to find out, then turned the corner and headed for home, four blocks away.

Rolly lived in a one-room granny flat above Highway 163, the old road that passed through the heart of Balboa Park into downtown San Diego. It wasn't much of a place, but the location couldn't be beat.

The iron light fixture over his front door was shining brightly when he arrived, making his humble abode look unusually cozy and warm. His mother, ever protective, had turned the light on for him. She lived in the two-story Victorian next door and rented the granny flat to him. It was a temporary business arrangement. They had agreed. That had been five years ago. He was still paying the same rent he had when he started, 200 dollars, which was a hell of a deal, considering the going rates in Hillcrest.

He opened the door, flicked on the light, and dropped the white paper bag on the table before crossing to the bedroom and sliding the guitar case under his bed. It was safe now. The rest of his guitars, currently ten of them, were kept in the living room, stacked in their cases, displayed in floor stands or hung on the wall. But the Gibson stayed under his bed, in a safe place, away from the eyes of the world.

He took off his shoes, walked back to the kitchen, sat down, and started to eat. There were still a lot of things in the world worth living for. One of them was a *carne asada* burrito at four in the morning.

CHAPTER 5

▼

WAKE UP CALL

Rolly lay in bed and stared at the ceiling. It was 6:32 A.M. He hadn't been able to sleep much. His stomach kept rumbling, perhaps from the *carne asada* burrito, but more likely from the uncomfortable thoughts in his head. Every time he closed his eyes, a picture of the man in the pool rose up in front of him.

He heard a car approach on the gravel driveway. Something thumped on the door. Rolly jumped, realized it was just the Sunday edition of the *Union-Tribune*. His chances for sleep seemed about over. He struggled out of bed, went to the kitchen, tried to decide which was worse, feeling old or hung over. As best he could tell, there wasn't much difference, but at least there was a cure for a hangover. There was a cure for getting old too, but it wasn't much of an option. The man in the pool might have been drunk, but he wouldn't have a hangover this morning.

Rolly put a few heaping tablespoons of coffee into the brewing machine, poured in some water, and flipped on the switch. He opened the front door, found the morning paper propped up against it perfectly. If the new deliveryman had any speed on his throws, the Padres should give him a tryout. They could do worse. They probably would.

This morning, like most, was shrouded in light misty fog. It would burn off in a couple of hours, giving way to another oppressively bright, pleasant day in the sun. It had been the same kind of morning, the same kind of day every day for the last thirty-nine years, for the last 200, for all Rolly could tell. He remembered something resembling rain a year or so back, but it might have been something he'd seen in a movie. The weather in San Diego had been one of the few things in life he could depend on.

The thought of the dead man in the pool kicked back into his head like a bad rap song, riffing on dope, "bitches," and guns. He sat down at the kitchen table and looked through the paper, trying to chase the thought out of his mind. He checked out the sports section first, ran through the box scores. The Padres had lost again. Their chances of repeating the pennant run of last year were already fading. He leafed through the world news, then the local section, thinking there might be a story about the man in the pool, but there was nothing. It didn't surprise him. Any police report that had been filed would have come in too late to make last night's deadline. But if someone had drowned at a millionaire mansion in The Farms, it would make the paper sooner or later.

The coffee machine sputtered, spit out a last gasp of caffeinated water. There was someone outside on the porch.

"Rolly?" It was a high sing-song voice. "Rolly, are you there? I've got some croissants for you." It was his mother.

"Come on in, Mom," Rolly yelled through the door.

The door opened like an apology. Rolly's mother walked in, her long gray hair pulled up in a loose bun. She had on a canary yellow nightshirt, which was tied gracefully at the waist above khaki pants and Japanese house slippers. She carried a small white paper sack in her right hand.

"It's a wonderful morning," she chirped, like an accusation. He never understood how someone could sound so cheerful and confrontational at the same time, as if she were daring him to disagree.

"Good morning, Mother," he shot back with the best attempt at enthusiasm he could muster. It was always tough to compete with his mother for the bright-eyed, bushy-tailed trophy, but for some reason he still tried. Maybe because if he didn't he risked the slow inquisition, even now, at thirty-nine. Even now, after he'd been sober for almost five years.

Rolly's flat stood behind his mother's house on Eighth Avenue, just south of Upas at the edge of Balboa Park. It was in the heart of Hillcrest, neighborhood home to members of the rainbow coalition, the hopelessly hip and the urban elderly. There were knick-knack shops, organic grocers, alternative bookstores, and chic restaurants and hair parlors. There wasn't a Hooters in sight.

His mother always said she moved to Hillcrest because it was "artistic." Rolly thought she moved there so she could flirt with attractive young men while avoiding the threat of any real sexual pressure. She liked attention. His father had never understood that. It was all she ever had wanted, just some attention, some hugs and some credit for taking care of their house and their son, who wasn't so easy to handle. Some credit for keeping herself almost celibate while her husband was away for six months at a time. Some credit for staying more honest then he ever had.

"You look tired," she said to him.

"I didn't get home until late."

"Did you have a good party?"

"It went pretty good. Rich people. Big house in The Farms, up on the cliffs above Black's. They seemed to like us pretty well."

"Well, perhaps there was someone there who could help your career. You never know with those folks in La Jolla. They've got connections."

Rolly's mother still thought of him as a full-time musician. He was never sure if she just liked to be encouraging or if she thought he still had a chance of making it big. He might be young in her eyes, but Rolly knew the guys in L.A. in the Armani suits and the $100 haircuts wouldn't even talk to you once you passed thirty-five. His mother never mentioned his day job, as if she pretended it didn't exist.

"You want some coffee?" Rolly said.

"Just half a cup, thank you dear." His mother sat down at the table. "How about some plates?"

Left to his own devices, Rolly avoided china and silverware whenever possible. It wasn't possible now. He poured out two mugs of coffee, went back to the kitchen, pulled out a couple of plates and two knives, brought them back to the table.

"So tell me more," said his mother, doling out a large croissant for each of them.

"Well, like I said, it was a nice house, right on the edge of the cliffs. Lots of big windows. You could see down to The Cove and up to Mt. Soledad. You could probably see all the way up to Dana Point on a clear day. And, of course, lots of ocean."

"I don't think I'd do anything all day if I had that kind of view. I'd just sit there and look out the window. Whose house was it?"

"I don't really know. They don't seem to live in it much. There must have been twenty rooms, but only a couple of them had any furniture. The party was outside on the patio, by the pool." There was that picture again in his head.

"Perhaps the owners are still moving in."

"Maybe. Fender said they hadn't been living there long."

"Fender lives there?"

"No, he just gave us a tour. He works for the company."

"Oh. What's the company called?"

"Eyebitz.com. It's an Internet company."

"Oh, yes. I think I've read about them. So Fender works for them?'

"Yes. He seems to think he's going to make a lot of money."

"Well, that's nice for him. I haven't seen Fender in years. He was always a nice boy. Shy and quiet, but very polite."

They continued their small talk a few minutes until they had finished their breakfast. His mother cleared the table and rinsed off the dishes while Rolly finished his coffee.

"I'm going to Henry's Market this morning," his mother said. "Can I get you anything while I'm there?"

"No, thanks, Mom. I'll go to Ralph's later," Rolly replied.

"That produce at Ralph's is full of chemicals and pesticide. You should go to Henry's. It's better for you."

"Maybe I will." He wasn't going to argue. He wasn't going to the grocery store, anyway. He hardly ever bought groceries. Sometimes he bought milk, cereal, coffee, maybe peanut butter and jelly, a loaf of bread.

His mother dried her hands on the towel by the sink. "Well, have a nice day, dear. Take a nap if you need to. You'll feel better."

"Thanks, Mom. Maybe I will."

His mother walked to the door, closed it softly behind her, leaving the room as empty as it had been before she arrived. Outside in the driveway, Rolly could hear a car pulling in, the gravel scrunching under its wheels. He stared into his coffee. The scrunching stopped. A car door opened and shut.

"Fender Simmons, is that you?" Rolly's mother sang out in a bright cheery chirp.

"Hello, Mrs. Waters. How are you?"

"Well I'm fine, Fender. I haven't seen you in years. Rolly tells me you're going to be very successful."

"I hope so, Mrs. Waters." Rolly could hear the puff of pride in Fender's voice, even through the door. "I think I may have hooked up with something really special."

"That's wonderful, Fender. How's your wife?" Rolly had neglected to tell his mother that Fender's marriage of last year had only lasted three months.

"My wife and I are separated, Mrs. Waters."

"Oh. I'm sorry to hear that, Fender."

Rolly was going to go crazy if his mother kept repeating Fender's name every time she said something to him. He didn't know why, but it bugged him. He got up from the table and opened the door.

CHAPTER 6

▼

A REQUEST

There was a forest green Ford Fiesta parked outside. Fender stood beside it, looking uncomfortable, trying to decide how much longer he needed to be polite before he disengaged himself from Rolly's mother. He tugged on his right ear, cleared his throat, tapped his left rear pants pocket as if to make sure his wallet was there. He had on a blue business shirt and brown pants, clunky black dress shoes. He stood for a second looking down at his feet, placing his hand on his forehead and stroking his eyebrows with thumb and forefinger.

"Hey, Fender," Rolly called out from the doorway.

"Hey, Rolly," Fender said in relief. He turned toward Rolly, smoothed his eyebrows again, then glanced back at Rolly's mother.

"Good to see you, Mrs. Waters."

"Good to see you, Fender," she said. "Rolly, are you sure you don't want anything from Henry's?"

"No, thanks, Mom." His mother walked away, carrying her canvas grocery bag, off on another big adventure amongst the organic fruits and vegetables.

"Come on in, Fender," Rolly said.

Fender rolled a shoulder, touched his hand to his back pocket again and walked in the door.

"Great party last night," Rolly said.

"Sure was," said Fender, regaining his enthusiasm. "Everybody loved the band. Ricky said you were one of the best bands he'd ever heard, couldn't believe you were from San Diego. He couldn't believe you weren't a big rock star."

Rolly kind of doubted Ricky had said anything about the band, but he appreciated Fender's kiss-up anyway. Of course, with Fender, a compliment was often followed by a request, a proposition. Rolly appreciated getting the gig, but with Fender there was always a marker to be paid. He wondered if Fender had heard anything about the man in the pool.

"So what do you want?" Rolly said.

Fender took a tiny step back, as if losing his balance. Directness in speech was always a little difficult for him to handle. But Rolly wanted to get to the point. If Fender got going on something, you'd never get another word in until you just gave up and agreed to whatever he was proposing.

Fender sat down in the faded leather easy chair. Rolly sat back at the table, took a sip on his coffee.

"I need to talk to you about something. It's important. The company needs your help." Fender's voice dropped a notch as he said "company," making it sound weighty and important. He stared at the floor as if to add gravitas.

"What is it?"

"We, the company I mean, would like to hire you for an investigation." He put a hand on either side of his temples, looked up from the deep eye sockets that gave him the appearance Moogus called the "Frankenstein look."

Red lights started flashing in Rolly's head like a squad car convention on F Street. He'd seen a dead man last night. The company the dead man worked for wanted to hire him. Companies never hired him, especially big, rich companies like Eyebitz.com. They hired investigators from big agencies, guys that knew certain guys because they'd worked for other rich guys' lawyers. Guys with money to spend, who subscribed to fifty-thousand-a-year information services and hired interns to do their research. Rolly found lost sailors and their ex-girlfriends for frightened mothers from Des Moines who just wanted them to come home. He spied on the wives of jealous North Park shop owners when they checked into tourist motels in Mission Valley with their biker boyfriends.

"I've got a check," Fender said.

"A check?"

"For you, it's a retainer. Private investigators always get a retainer, right? That's what they do in the movies." Fender rolled the fingers on his right hand. He was nervous, which set Rolly at ease. It was only Fender he had to deal with for now.

"Sure, I like to have a retainer. But tell me what you want first. How do you know I'm the right person for the job?" Rolly tried to sound professional, whatever professional was.

"We can't take this to the police. We need someone we can trust. We can't have it in the papers. So first you have to tell me that anything I say won't leave this room."

"By my girlfriend's butt and all that's holy," said Rolly, reciting an old joke between them. Fender snarfed a nervous laugh.

"Okay, Rolly. By Leslie's butt and all that's holy." It was Moogus' line, but Fender liked to use it. Fender had always been hot for Leslie, Rolly's longtime girlfriend, ex-girlfriend now. She thought Fender was creepy, a total loser. But Fender didn't know that. Leslie did have a behind to die for.

"There's an item missing from our offices. We don't know if it's stolen or just missing," Fender continued.

"What is it?"

"It's a key."

"Can't you just replace the lock and get a new one?"

"It's not that kind of key. It's part of the computer system."

"What computer system?"

"Well, I can't explain it completely, it's kind of technical. I don't completely understand it, myself. Ricky can explain it to you."

"Ricky?"

"Yeah, he'd like to see you as soon as possible. He wants to talk to you in person. I just wanted to check with you first, see if you could do the job."

"Why me?"

"I told Ricky you could do it. He liked you. He said you seemed like someone he could trust." Rolly wasn't sure he bought that one. Nobody ever thought of a rock and roll guitar player as someone they could trust. Someone they could screw over and cheat maybe, not someone they trusted.

Fender reached into his back pocket, pulled out an envelope with the Eyebitz.com logo on it. He opened the envelope, handed a check over to Rolly. It was a blank check with Ricky's signature on it. Rolly put it down on the table, turned back to Fender.

"It's a blank check."

"Like I said, Ricky trusts you. Whatever you think the retainer should be, you just fill it out."

"Are you sure somebody didn't just drop the key between some sofa cushions? What if they find it tomorrow?"

"You can keep the retainer, either way. Ricky says he trusts you to do the right thing. He says you've got a high integrity quotient. But you have to meet with him today, this morning. It's very urgent."

Rolly listened, but he was thinking about the last time someone had written him a blank check. Fender had been there. Five years ago at Capitol Records, an Artist & Repertoire man had pushed a blank check across his desk to Rolly and Matt, the lead singer in Rolly's band, and Rolly's friend. It was an investment in their talent, the A&R man said, an advance on their sure-to-happen stardom. It was their shot at the big gold ring. Matt and Rolly took the check, shook hands with the A&R guy. Fender slept outside in the car. Fender always hung out with Rolly and Matt, following them around like a pet beagle. Rolly walked to the liquor store across Vine Street, picked up a pint of Jack Daniels and a six-pack of Bud, brought it back to the car to share with Fender and Matt. They started celebrating. They drove home, taking the scenic route, stopping at every bar they found along old Highway 101. Then came the accident.

Maybe this offer from Fender was a kind of second chance, a little return on Rolly's recent years of good behavior, a reward for his repentance. If he did well, he could move onto bigger cases, start to work with companies and corporations instead of greasy, beer-breathed mechanics trying to find a missing girlfriend and the rebuilt '71 Camaro she'd taken with her. Or the lost teenagers he'd find for squabbling parents who probably hadn't wanted to have kids in the first place. Maybe it was time to try being ambitious again. There was the guy in the pool to think about, too.

At any rate, it couldn't hurt to meet with Ricky. It wasn't really a contract until you cashed the check. At least that's how the A&R guy at Capitol Records had explained it to Matt and Rolly.

He picked up the check on the kitchen table, folded it over. "Okay, I'll talk to him. Can I take a quick shower?"

"Sure. Thanks, Rolly."

Rolly walked back to the bedroom, pulled off the extra large t-shirt he'd slept in, and walked into the bathroom. The big cloud in his head had just gotten bigger and was threatening rain. He looked at himself in the mirror, his middle-aged body, round, pink, and naked. A blank check from someone he'd only just met, someone who pulled in dollar bills as if they were sunbeams. It meant complicating his life when he was trying to keep things simple.

He showered, changed his clothes, put on a pair of khakis, something resembling a dress shirt, and a tan jacket. When he walked back into the living room, Fender was strumming "Sunshine of Your Love" on Rolly's green Stratocaster.

The case lay open on the floor in the living room. Fender was a hopelessly mediocre guitar player, but an earnest one.

"Hey Rolly, what was that guitar you were playing last night? It looked cool."

"That's my ES-335. I keep it under my bed. I don't feel safe if it's out of my sight." He was about to mention leaving it at the party, but stopped himself just in time. It wasn't a good idea to tell anyone about last night, even Fender. Especially Fender. Because Fender couldn't keep a secret if you sewed his mouth shut and dropped him in a cement hole. He was just naturally talkative.

Rolly grabbed his keys, turned off the coffee pot. "All right then. Let's go."

CHAPTER 7

▼

THE HIDDEN FORTRESS

Rolly followed Fender's car north on Highway 5, taking the exit at Genesee Avenue, north of UCSD, where the smart kids went to college. The smart white kids and the smart Asian kids. They were the ones, mostly, who were learning to build the next big thing, be it software or pharmaceuticals, designer DNA, some scary and complicated technology that would make the smart kids a million dollars someday.

Just before they reached Torrey Pines Road, Fender took a right on Atomic Way (named in a time when another technology pushed at the edge of the world's problems, scaring people to death). Rolly followed.

They pulled up to a long metal gate. Fender rolled down his window, reached out, and punched in a few numbers on the keypad.

"Stay right behind me," Fender yelled back. "The gate closes slow, so two cars can get through if you hurry." He waved. Rolly waved back. They drove up a small asphalt incline, pulled left into the parking lot. There were about two dozen cars in the lot, too many for a Sunday. Apparently, these folks never took a day off, even with the hangovers some of them must have had from last night.

The building itself was the standard industrial-park box, a big two-story rectangle, with a square tinted window every twenty feet, top and bottom.

They walked to the entrance. Fender pulled on the metal handle of the large glass door. It was locked. He looked in, saw the guard looking out at him. Fender felt around in his pockets.

"Oh, hell. Where's my security card?" He flopped around some more, waved at the guard. The guard got up from his desk and walked over, opened the door.

"Thanks, Sonny," said Fender. "Don't know where I left my card."

Sonny looked like he'd heard the story before. He didn't care.

"Sign the temporary form. You, sir, sign in too, please," he said, pointing Rolly towards a clipboard on the front desk. Rolly filled in the information— name and phone. He paused at the line that read "reason for visit."

"What's my reason for visiting?"

"Just say you're meeting with Ricky," Fender said.

The guard handed Rolly a security card. It had a belt clip attached to the top and the word "VISITOR" printed in large black letters over the Eyebitz.com logo. The guard gave a card to Fender, as well. It read "DUNCE CAP", with a little cartoon figure faced into a corner, wearing a tall cone-shaped hat.

"I shouldn't have lost my card," Fender said. "The security's tight here. It has to be. The proprietary technology we have could be worth millions, billions even, Ricky says."

"Who's idea was that?" Rolly said, pointing to the dunce cap figure drawing.

"Ricky's. I'm going to go see him now, let him know you're here. Wait here in the lobby. I'll come and get you."

Rolly sat down in a lipstick-red chair with a high back that flew off in a wing shape at one end. He looked around the lobby. The floor was pink marble, or possibly granite. There were fake marble columns on either side of the guard's desk, a hallway leading back to what looked like a mural from Chicano Park, and a stairway going up to the second floor. Lamps on the wall were held up by small plaster gargoyles, painted black and silver. Above Rolly's head hung a huge stylized eye, the Eyebitz.com corporate logo, in brushed stainless steel, trimmed in black, and threatening to drop any moment, crushing him or anyone else trapped in the lobby.

Rolly picked up a brochure that lay on the table next to his chair. The brochure was printed in glossy purple and yellow, with another big Eyebitz.com logo on the cover. Inside were black and white photographs of young people. Rolly read the accompanying text:

> *Eyebitz.com is at the forefront of the enablization of a new marketplace, allowing the global exchange of ideas to emerge by extending media supply chain synergies to creative professionals and clients through the unique power of the Internet.*

Rolly wondered if enablization was a real word.

Using the power of data, our media delivery services create a new marketplace for artists, filmmakers, musicians, and writers to promote their work to a global audience, unencumbered by the restrictions and contradictions of the media power elite.

There was more.

Analyze. Categorize. Customize.
Words. Pictures. Music.
Find the words that focus you. Play the song that pleases you. Watch the scenes that wow you.

Somebody was working overtime on the alliteration, but it wasn't making things any clearer. He tried another section, under "Our Technology."

Eyebitz.com presents eSurf®, the next wave on the Internet. eSurf® is cutting-edge technology for analyzing and processing data in order to compare customer choices, habits, and preferences.

By using recursive algorithmic processing and iWatcher® technology, the system helps guide user decisions and provides faster and more effective access to content. It helps content providers identify their customers through thin-channel targeted marketing. The more a user listens, the more a user watches, the more eSurf® knows about the user's interests and taste. Advertising and ideas are pushed to the user through the framing of the traditional browser in eSurf®, which provides a seamless, organic web experience.

eSurf® from Eyebitz.com. Creating trends before the trend. Riding the perfect power wave.

Rolly looked up from his reading and saw two feminine feet, strapped in black high heels, descending the staircase. They were followed by incredibly long legs, covered up at the last minute by a black leather miniskirt. It was Alesis. She had on a green silk blouse, draped over a more professional bosom than she'd displayed at the party last night, more intimidating but still inviting.

"Mr. Waters. I'm Alesis Amati. Mr. Rogers is available to meet with you now."

As Rolly followed Alesis up the stairs, he found himself facing her leathered backside, compared it briefly with the memory of Leslie's, then looked away, reminding himself to stay focused on the business at hand. Alesis gave no indication she even remembered him.

"Would you like anything to drink?" she asked. "Coffee, tea, soft drinks, juice?"

"I'm fine," said Rolly, breathing heavily, either from stress, or the view, or from climbing the stairs, probably all of them. He hoped Alesis hadn't noticed his wheezing.

They turned down a hall at the top of the stairs and passed a set of publicity photographs, most of which seemed to be autographed. Rolly recognized a few faces, local lounge singers, infommercial pitchmen, and cable T.V. personalities. Many of the pictures were signed, "To Ricky."

"You look familiar," Alesis said. "Have we met before?"

"Well, I was at the party last night," Rolly said. She looked at him again, as if trying to remember. She had dark green eyes like a cat's.

"I played in the band."

"Oh yes, of course," she said. "The man who rocked Japan." She didn't sound quite convinced, though, as if she were trying to remember something else.

They stopped at a door with a printed brass plaque. It said Ricky Rogers, CVO. Inside the room, someone was yelling. Alesis wrinkled her nose, gave a small, apprehensive sigh before knocking on the door. The yelling stopped.

CHAPTER 8

▼

THE CVO

"Who is it?"

"Ricky, it's Alesis. I've got Mr. Waters here."

A moment passed. The door opened to reveal Fender standing just inside. Beyond Fender, sitting at a large desk facing them was Ricky, who was looking at something on his computer. There was an older man, Alesis' ex, the one who had been trying to find his glasses at the party. He sat on a leather sofa across the room from Ricky, inspecting his fingernails. Rolly entered the room. Alesis closed the door behind him.

Fender got things started. "Ricky, this is Rolly Waters, the private investigator I told you about."

"I know who he is, Fender. You told me. And Alesis just told me, too. Everyone in the fucking building has told me now." Ricky continued to stare at his computer monitor, tapping aggressively at the keyboard.

This was a different version of Ricky than the one Rolly had met last night, the one who'd been all smiles and hale fellow. This Ricky was wound up so tight he was going to explode if you tapped him just right, like one of those old artillery shells left by the Marines in an East County canyon, dug up by a construction crew as they started a new housing development.

"I've been told you can help us," Ricky said, still focused on his computer screen. Rolly imagined bright red laser beams shooting out from Ricky's eyes, drilling a hole through the glass screen, into the metal and plastic inside.

"Well, I hope I can help," Rolly said. Ricky was bearing down on the computer monitor like a freckled coyote chasing a gopher down into its hole.

"Hope is for idiots," Ricky said. "I don't hire idiots."

There was a time in his life when a guy like this would have set Rolly off, brought his own anger up to the surface. But if Rolly got angry, he'd want a drink. That's how he used to handle his anger. He was recovering now, from assholes as well as alcohol. He'd learned how to cope. He took a deep breath, counted to five under his breath. He counted again. The only way he knew to make the world work when it spun up too fast was to bring it back down to a speed he could manage. If it meant other people found him a little slow, so be it.

"What I mean is, I'd like to know a little more about the problem before I commit to taking the case."

Ricky took a last, vicious tap at his keyboard, turned to look directly at Rolly.

"Mr. Waters, we don't have problems here at Eyebitz.com. What we have are opportunities. What we have are solutions that remain unfound. That's the whole philosophy this company is built on."

Ricky zapped Rolly with a big smile. It was the same smile, with the practiced-to-perfection look of assertion in his eye, that he'd given Rolly last night when they were introduced. It rolled across Rolly like a big wave at Black's Beach. He rolled with it, kept himself grounded. After the wave comes the undertow. It sucks away all the sand under your feet.

"Fender has explained a little to me. Can you tell me more about this Magic Key I'm supposed to find?"

"Yes I can. But before I do that, let me ask you what you know about our business. Do you understand what we do?"

"Well, I've read a little in the newspaper, and I read the brochure downstairs while I was waiting."

"And how would you describe our business?"

"Well, you have some sort of computerized audio video service. From what I understand, that means you can send video over the Internet to people's computers. According to your brochure, you send it better than anyone else."

"And …?"

"And you can track what people are watching. And because you track what they're watching, you can sell them exactly what they want."

"Is that it?"

"In fifty words or less, that's about the best I can do."

Ricky smiled. It was a little smile this time, directed inward. He dropped his eyes down towards his desk, winding up for his pitch like Randy Johnson on the mound at Qualcomm Stadium, ready to blow another one past some feeble Padres' batter.

"What we're really selling, Mr. Waters, is the future. And we have to get to the future faster than anyone else. We have to make our future *the* future. And in order to make our future happen, we have to protect it tightly so no one else gets there first."

Ricky had practiced this pitch so many times, it almost sounded like he was making sense. Rolly said nothing, acted like he was processing the information. He wasn't going to say anything unless he had to. He was miles outside of his comfort zone right now.

"Let me get down to details," continued Ricky. "Do you know what an algorithm is?"

"Something to do with math?" Rolly said, taking a swing, hoping to at least foul one off the end of his bat.

"Yes, it has something to do with math. An algorithm is, in fact, a mathematical formula used to process a computer event. This company is based on a set of algorithms, created by Curtis Vox, our chief technology officer. The algorithms he created are used to encode our digital content."

"Sounds good," Rolly said, not feeling too bright. He looked over at Fender, wondered if Fender understood any of this. Fender was fiddling with his temporary badge, the one with the dunce cap drawn on it.

"It's very good," Ricky said, bearing down. "But what's more important is we've created a way to track how people respond to the content we send them. Let me show you something."

Ricky turned back to his computer and waved Rolly over next to him. He clicked the mouse and the screen went black. After another second or two, it popped back to life. There was a Japanese cartoon in the center of the screen, with advertisements displayed in a rectangular box around the outer edges of the cartoon. There was an ad for Coca-Cola, one for Subaru, some others Rolly didn't recognize.

"As I watch the video here, I can also click any of these graphics. When I click I get more information," Ricky said. He clicked on the Coca Cola logo. The logo animated, spun around, and flipped over. It now said, "Win a Hawaiian Holiday."

"Hmm," Rolly said, trying to sound impressed, as if he were seeing the future Ricky wanted him to.

"But here's the critical part, Mr. Waters. Information flows both ways. As a user watches the video, we can watch the user. Everything the user does on screen while the video is playing gets recorded and sent back to our servers. For instance, we can know that at one minute, thirteen seconds into this cartoon, a certain user has clicked on the Coca-Cola logo. We can then store the information in our database, analyze patterns and predict user behavior, allowing us to target advertising for our sponsors in ever more accurate ways. Isn't that fantastic?"

It sounded more creepy than fantastic to Rolly, like something out of George Orwell. He decided to keep that opinion to himself.

"This key that's missing. What does it have to do with any of this?"

"Like I said, it's the Magic Key," Ricky said.

"What's magic about it?"

"Inside this building is a locked, secured room and inside that room is a magic box, a special computer on which we run the algorithms that are key to our eSurf technology. That computer is not connected to any other computers in the building."

"And you've lost the key to the room?"

"Oh, I have a key to the room. It's right here," Ricky said, holding up his security card. It was just like the one Rolly and Fender had, except it was red. "This gets me into the room. I have one. Curtis has one. And King here has one," Ricky said, nodding towards the bald man on the sofa, who was still concentrating on his cuticles.

"I'm guess I still don't understand what this Magic Key is."

"The Magic Key isn't a room key. It's a removable data disk that connects to the computer in that room. If the disk isn't connected to the computer, the eSurf algorithms won't run. The disk is encrypted with part of the algorithm that makes eSurf work. By keeping the algorithm in separate pieces, we protect it. All of our engineers have access to the first part of the algorithm. But you need both pieces to make the system fully functional. If someone had the Magic Key and was able to get into the computer room, they would have access to all of our technology. They could steal all our secrets. Those algorithms are the lifeblood of this company. They're worth millions, possibly billions someday."

"I don't really know much about computers," Rolly said. "Perhaps you should consider hiring someone who does."

Ricky smiled. "Mr. Waters, you have just confirmed my initial opinion of your integrity and character. Your honesty and forthrightness are exactly the reasons I think we should hire you."

"Well, I do have other clients right now," Rolly lied, looking for ways to avoid making a commitment, wanting to buy himself time to think about what he was getting into.

"I understand that," Ricky said, "we'll make it worth your time, financially. What do you charge?"

"Five hundred dollars a day, plus expenses," Rolly replied, making a concerted effort not to blink. It wasn't a lie. His rate card said five hundred a day. But he'd never been paid at that rate. The clients he worked for could barely manage fifty a day.

Ricky nodded to the older man on the sofa. "Mr. Gibson here handles our finances. King, what do you think?"

"Seven-fifty a day, plus ten thousand in options," Gibson said, without looking up from his fingernails.

"Options?" Rolly said.

"Certainly, Mr. Waters," said Ricky. "As a temporary contractor with our company, we like to consider you part of the family. We're willing to offer you ten thousand in option shares above and beyond your daily fee."

"You mean stock options?"

"Yes, as you may know, we intend to take this company public by the end of next month. If you accept our offer, those options will be worth considerably more when that happens. How much are our shares priced at now, King?"

"Exactly one dollar."

"So your ten thousand shares are worth ten thousand dollars today, Mr. Waters. A nice even number. If our IPO goes anywhere near as well as planned, you could make that ten, twenty, even thirty times over."

"Just for finding the Magic Key?"

"Just for finding the Magic Key and returning it to us."

Rolly's head was swimming. His stomach was churning. He liked to pretend that he didn't care about money, that he was happy with life just the way it was. It was his recovery mantra. *Keep things simple. Don't get in over your head.*

He looked at the faces around him, Ricky's eyes boring into him brightly, King Gibson in silent contemplation of his cuticles, and Fender, silently pleading with Rolly to make him look good with the boss.

"Let me just ask plainly, Mr. Waters, will you help us with our problem?" Ricky asked, still pressing. He was the kind of man who never stopped pressing.

Five years ago, Rolly's life had almost ended. He'd screwed up his chance for grabbing the big gold ring. Leslie had left him. Matt had been killed. Rolly had dropped into a hole so deep that he thought he'd never get out. But he'd finally stopped drinking. He'd started playing guitar again, writing songs. And he'd obtained his P.I. license. Perhaps this was one more rung in the ladder leading out of the hole he'd dug for himself, something he could grab onto to get himself clear.

He looked back at Ricky, as directly as he could manage, trying to return a little wattage in kind.

"Ricky," he said, "I think this is an opportunity, not a problem."

"Yes, an opportunity." Ricky smiled. "Welcome aboard, Mr. Waters. Mr. Gibson will draw up the papers."

So that was it. The business was done. Ricky's confident ways were contagious. Rolly decided it was his turn to take charge.

"So when did you last see the key?" he asked.

"Curtis reported it missing. He emailed me this morning."

"Who is Curtis again?"

"Curtis Vox is our Chief Technology Officer. He created the algorithms. He's the man with the technical skills."

"He's in charge of the key?"

"Yes."

"And he lost it?"

"Apparently. Or someone stole it from him."

"I should talk to him. Is he here?"

"No, but we'll have him contact you when we find him."

"He's missing too?"

"Not exactly, but Mr. Vox is often hard to get hold of. Curtis is a genius, the brains, the heart and soul of this company. He keeps his own agenda and we try not to impose an artificial schedule on him."

"That seems kind of unusual."

"Curtis is not your usual employee, Mr. Waters. Eyebitz.com is not your usual company. There's a new way of doing business now, a "new wave," I like to call it."

"Well, I do think I should talk to him."

"Of course."

"And this computer, the one in the room. Perhaps I should take a look at it so I can get some idea of what I'm looking for."

"Of course."

Ricky withdrew his attention from Rolly and returned to his computer, scowled, entered another room in his mind, shutting the rest of them out. The interview was over.

CHAPTER 9

▼

THE ZOO

Rolly waited a moment, unsure. Fender shot a glance at him from behind his deep eye sockets and then looked towards the door. Rolly took the hint and walked out, closing the door behind him. Alesis was sitting at her desk, right hand on her chin, index finger extended and touching her nose. She was reading a big glossy magazine titled *Italia*. She looked even better than she had twenty minutes ago.

"How'd it go?" She smiled at him.

"Well, if you mean, did I get the job, I guess it went fine." Rolly was still thinking about what it really meant. He felt woozy, a little bit giddy. Thirty times ten thousand. That was three hundred thousand dollars.

"What else would I mean?" Alesis said.

"I don't know."

"Well, when you figure it out, you can give me a call."

Maybe he would give her a call. She probably had options, too. Maybe they could get together sometime and compare their options. He understood it was all the rage among the young professionals these days, sitting at Starbuck's, trading stock tips and sipping their lattes.

"Planning a trip?" Rolly said, indicating the magazine.

"Someday. I'm hoping. Venice and Florence and Rome. I'd like to stay in one of these villas someday." She held out a photograph. "I'm planning to use some of the money I'll get from selling my stock."

"Sounds good."

"It's either that or marry a rich geek."

"Geek?"

"You know, nerds, the guys who work with computers. They're the ones who really make the big money."

"Plenty of them around here, I guess. How do you feel about musicians?"

"Rich or poor?"

"In transition."

"It all depends on which direction they're headed."

"But you don't rule them out?"

"I don't rule out any man who's got money."

The door to Ricky's office opened and Fender stepped out. "Rolly, you're still here. Good. Ricky asked me to show you around, help you get started."

The intercom on Alesis' desk buzzed.

"Yes, Ricky," she said.

"Alesis, is Mr. Waters still here?"

"Yes, he's standing right in front of me."

"Well, King thinks you should give him a tour around the building. Let him have a look around, whatever he wants to see, including the lockup room."

"Sure, Ricky. But I thought Fender was going to show him around."

There was a pause. Fender's jaw seemed to lock up. It looked like he was trying to swallow an egg.

"Fender can go with you, too."

The egg slipped down, disappeared from Fender's throat. Alesis got up from her chair, gave her skirt a quick tug to keep things properly covered.

"All right, Mr. Waters. It looks like you'll have both of us for company. What would you like to see first?"

"I guess the standard tour. I'd like to get the lay of the land first."

Alesis frowned at him for a split second, as if she thought there might be an insinuation somewhere in his remark. She relaxed, seemed to decide there wasn't an insult intended and started back down the hall. She'd probably heard her share of smart cracks from men with bad manners, but Rolly wasn't one of them.

"Follow me, boys," she said. "We'll go to Rohan first."

"Rohan?" Rolly asked Fender.

"Oh, it's from that book," Fender said, "you know, the Hobbits and Elves."

"*Lord of the Rings?*"

"Yeah, that's it. Curtis came up with it. The engineers are the Hobbits. Marketing people like me, we're the Elves. We live in Rohan."

"You're pretty tall for an elf," Rolly said. Fender shrugged his shoulders.

They walked down the hall past the top of the stairs to the other end the building. There were more plaster gargoyles hanging on the wall and a large jagged piece of bent metal that had been twisted, warped, and distressed just enough by some artist to make it worth thousands of dollars, Rolly guessed. They walked past the sharp-edged sculpture and continued down the hall.

"What does CVO stand for?" Rolly asked Fender.

"CVO?"

"Yeah, I've heard of CEOs. But on Ricky's door it said CVO."

"Oh, that. It stands for Chief Vision Officer. Ricky doesn't like to use traditional titles. He says it's limiting."

And Ricky was not a man to admit he had limits, thought Rolly. At least not in front of his employees.

"This is our marketing department," Alesis said, waving her hand as they entered a large open room. The room contained two flimsy fold-out tables placed end to end. Alesis paused just like a real tour guide, allowing Rolly to take in the scene.

A dozen or so young men and women sat at the tables, crammed into folding chairs, facing computers. They were all talking loudly, but apparently not to each other. Rolly looked closer and saw they were all wearing tiny headsets attached to cell phones. The cell phones lay on the table or were clipped to their belts. A heady sense of excitement filled the room, enthusiasm mixed with a faint whiff of desperation. These people were so close to making it big they could taste it, so close they were willing to work on a Sunday, ready to sacrifice every waking hour to make it happen, afraid they might fall behind, miss their chance. It was intoxicating, a mixture so rich you could get sick on it, like a kid rushing to finish his Halloween candy before his parents threw it away, or a drunk begging extra drinks from the bartender just after last call. Rolly felt caught up in the excitement in spite of himself.

Every few seconds, a person at one of the tables would get up, hurry over to another side of the table, talk intently for a few seconds with someone else in the room, then step away from the table and start talking again into thin air. A swirling energy filled the space as its occupants orbited the tables, spun off like random electrons. They switched positions without any recognizable pattern, forming new nuclei, then broke apart again and returned to their initial positions.

"I've got my own office," Fender said, pointing towards the corner of the room. There was a row of office doors running along the opposite wall. They walked over to the last door. Pinned to the wall outside the door was a handwritten sign on lined paper. It said "Fender Simmons, V.P.—Promotional Incentives." Fender and Rolly looked inside.

"Hey, Derek, hey, Rod!" Fender called out to the occupants of the room. The two young men inside focused deeply on their computer screens, as if they expected to find thousand-dollar bills hidden inside. They grunted at Fender without looking up. Another computer stood in the corner, surrounded on three sides by piles of paper and marketing detritus—t-shirts, bumper stickers, and Eyebitz.com-inscribed coffee mugs.

"That's my desk there," Fender said, pointing at an empty spot amongst the piles of junk.

"V.P., huh? Not bad," Rolly said. "What does 'Promotional Incentives' mean?"

"I'm in charge of creating mindshare."

"Oh," Rolly said. Another non-traditional title and job description from Ricky, no doubt.

"A lot of V.P.s in this part of the building," Alesis said, almost under her breath.

"They won't talk to you if you're not a V.P.," Fender said, sounding a little wounded. "If you just call up a client and tell them you're Joe Schmo, salesman, they hang up on you. They'll wait if you're a V.P. They'll wait and listen to what you've got to say. You get to define your own destiny."

Alesis rolled her eyes. She turned and started walking again.

"This way, gentlemen. Next stop, the Zoo."

"The zoo?" Rolly asked.

"The nerds, the geeks," Alesis said. "That's where we keep them."

"I thought they were Hobbits."

"Whatever," Alesis replied, "I call it the Zoo."

They walked back to the stairway, down to the lobby, past the guard's desk towards the back of the building. They took a left down another hallway, this one painted deep red, with more gargoyles and framed headshots. Before long they came to another large room. It was open also, with an uncovered ceiling that displayed gigantic steel beams, electrical conduit, and ventilation ducts. The floor of the room was divided into two sets of small offices, a large open space between them. The offices were built out of translucent white plastic hung on aluminum framing. They were dark inside except for the soft phosphorous glow of computer screens, which illuminated the faces of the occupants, casting shadows as if they were ghosts.

"This is it," Alesis said, pausing for effect. "The Zoo."

In the large open space between the plastic enclosures, there were heavily padded sofas and chairs like the ones in the lobby. Two of the chairs had been turned over, and from behind each of them two young men, armed with toy guns, faced off against each other in some sort of shootout. Little plastic pellets flew through the air like a scene from a Hong Kong gangster movie. Three other men, barefoot, wearing shorts and beach shirts, were tossing a Frisbee, leaping to catch it while diving over one of the sofas, crashing softly on the cushions as they fell. Alesis forged ahead. Rolly followed her, heard a yell. He ducked as an errant throw of the Frisbee flew by his face. The disc glanced off Fender's ear and fell to the floor.

"Sorry," sang out one of the Frisbee tossers, a skinny pale kid, who didn't look a day over eighteen, with glasses and a tattoo of what looked like a penguin on his arm. Fender picked up the Frisbee, tossed it back with an errant wobble. Alesis slowed her gait, added the tiniest wiggle. It was enough. The action halted as the boys stopped to watch her pass. One leapt on a chair, crouching and pining like a lonely raccoon.

"My little code monkeys," Alesis said. "That's what I like to call them." She sounded motherly, but that little hip action Rolly had seen wasn't so motherly.

"What do they do?" Rolly asked.

"They're the programmers, the guys that work on the software," Fender chimed in.

They reached the other side of the room, took a right around the corner of one line of white plastic boxes, passed by the open doorways of the offices. In each one, the occupant was playing what looked like the same computer game, blasting away at camouflaged monsters. The game players laughed and swore at each other through the translucent walls.

"Doesn't look like they're working much now," observed Rolly.

"The engineers set their own schedule," explained Fender. "Ricky says it's the wave of the future. Employees should define their own agenda." It sounded like a quote directly from Ricky's mouth.

"So where is this special computer, the one that uses the Magic Key?"

"We're almost there now," Alesis said.

They took another turn into a shorter hallway. There was a fire door at the end of it, sunlight peeking through at its seams. There were two rooms on their right. The first room was empty, except for a man who sat on the floor in a yoga position, eyes closed. He had dirty blonde hair and the largest hands Rolly had ever seen. He was dressed in baggy shorts and a Hawaiian t-shirt. He wore a puka shell necklace against his tanned skin.

"This is it," Alesis said as they stopped in front of the second door, which was closed. "You can see the computer up there." She pointed above the door, where a closed circuit T.V. monitor hung. On the screen was a fuzzy black and white picture of a plastic box, about two feet high, locked inside a metal cage. Small lights ran around the top of the cage, blinking in sequence.

"Well it looks pretty secure," Rolly said.

"That's only half of it," said Fender. "The computer casing has a special 'poison pill' feature. If you remove the cover the whole thing explodes."

"It explodes?" Rolly wanted to laugh. "Really?"

"That's what they tell us. Ricky says it's there to prevent reverse engineering."

"Well, I guess that would do it," Rolly said, not quite sure what reverse engineering was, but certain an exploding computer would help prevent it.

"Boys and their toys," Alesis said, rolling her eyes again. Rolly was beginning to like her attitude almost as much as her looks.

"Can we go in?" Rolly asked.

"We can't get in without Ricky's security card," Fender said. "Ricky or King has to be here."

"Or Curtis," Alesis said.

"Or Curtis."

"So tell me about Curtis. What's he like?"

Alesis and Fender glanced at each other, as if hoping the other would respond. Fender started.

"We don't really see him that much. He's kind of a super-geek."

"Ricky said he was hard to get hold of. Doesn't he come into work like everybody else?"

"No, he mostly stays out at the house," Alesis said.

"The house?"

"The BFH," Fender said. He looked down at the floor, twitching the dunce card between his index finger and thumb. Alesis shot an almost imperceptible glance over at Fender. There was something a little vicious in her eyes.

"I'm sorry," Rolly said, "I don't understand." Fender looked up at him.

"The house where the party was. Curtis lives there."

A hundred questions shot through Rolly's brain simultaneously, creating a hot, bubbly liquid that ran down his throat and swished around in his stomach. He saw a dark shadow floating across a swimming pool. Was Curtis dead? He couldn't be. Ricky said he had received an email from Curtis this morning. Had Curtis been at the house when Rolly found the man in the pool? He might have been.

"What does BFH mean?" Rolly said, trying to think of something to say to keep his composure. Alesis sighed.

"It means Big Fucking House," Alesis said. "Curtis likes to call it that. It's his idea of a funny joke."

The yoga man in the room they had passed started playing harmonica, blowing a slow, worn out blues riff. The guy wasn't half bad, but he wasn't exactly Sonny Boy Williamson either. Fender, Alesis, and Rolly stood in the hall looking at the picture of the computer on the television monitor and the blinking lights that surrounded it, the metal box that held the secrets of Eyebitz.com, the secrets that could only be unlocked with the Magic Key.

"Well, I don't really need to go in," Rolly said at last. "I'm afraid it's just a bunch of blinking lights to me." An exploding computer wasn't something he wanted to mess with right at the moment.

CHAPTER 10

▼

A DETOUR

For the third time in the last eighteen hours, Rolly found himself driving his old Volvo wagon out to The Farms. He was headed for the mansion on the cliffs, the BFH, in search of the elusive Eyebitz.com employee, Curtis Vox, the man who had emailed Ricky that morning to report that the Magic Key had gone missing. Rolly knew now, deep in his heart, that there was more to this whole thing than a lost disk. He knew he was in over his head. Because Curtis Vox surely knew something about a dead man floating in a swimming pool, even if no one else did.

Curtis Vox didn't own the mansion on the cliffs. According to Alesis, he was living there courtesy of a rich Eyebitz.com investor who owned the house. The investor lived in Mexico, rarely used the place.

Rolly felt a rough edge gnawing inside him now, an ugly excitement, like a rusty knife twisting inside his brain. It was the feeling he used to get when someone brought a bottle of Jack Daniels backstage before a gig. He tried to resist dangerous things, but somehow he couldn't.

He passed the granite monoliths at the entrance to The Farms. His nervousness started to scream. He found himself thinking of Leslie again. She lived with her husband one street away from where he was now. He passed the turn that would take him to the mansion and headed for Leslie's instead.

Leslie had stayed with Rolly through some of his worst years. She had put up with him when he was drunk, stoned, sleeping around. She had listened to him lie at eight o'clock in the morning, alcohol on his breath, the smell of other women on his shirt. She had been steadfast, supportive, and patient, like a beautiful mound of garden mulch. She gave him more chances in life than anyone else ever had. Except for one day when she hadn't, when she packed up her clothes and her fancy kitchen utensils and left him for good. It was the day before Rolly, Fender, and Matt went to L.A. to meet the man from Capitol Records.

Leslie lived with Joe now, her husband, a doctor. They owned an old California ranch house at the outer edge of The Farms, on a small canyon just off the private access road that led down to Black's Beach. They had two Labrador retrievers, a Siamese cat, and a parakeet. Leslie had a good life, better than anything she could have had with Rolly.

He found himself at Joe and Leslie's driveway. He turned in, all the time thinking this was a bad idea, wondering why he suddenly wanted to see her. He felt vaguely ashamed, like a man who couldn't let go of his past. He hoped Leslie was at home by herself. Joe wasn't a bad guy, downright decent, in fact, but Rolly wanted her all to himself. Seeing her might settle him down. Part of him wanted to brag, too, tell her he was working on something that was a big deal, legitimate. He wanted to tell her about the ten thousand option shares he was going to get.

But he wasn't going to have any luck today. Leslie's BMW was gone and Joe was standing outside, next to his Jaguar, throwing a tennis ball to the dogs. Once you started down the driveway, you had to go all the way in, make a loop in order to get back out. Joe saw him coming. Rolly had to say hi. He waved at Joe, pulled alongside the Jaguar, and rolled down the window.

Joe smiled. "Hey, Rolly, what brings you to the coast?" Joe was a doofus, a likable guy with a doctor's brain and a heart like a clear summer day. He worked up the road at the Scripps Clinic four days a week, tending to wealthy old ladies, and at a free clinic in San Ysidro one day a week, tending to children of poor Mexican immigrants. He spent all his free time and money on Leslie. Rolly wished that Leslie had married a jerk, so he could pretend he still had a chance of reclaiming her affection. But Joe was the hero. Rolly was the jerk.

"Hey, Joe. I had some business in the neighborhood. So I thought I'd stop by."

"Leslie's out." Joe picked up the tennis ball the dogs had dropped at his feet, threw it back out for them to retrieve again.

"Yeah, I figured."

They were silent a moment, watching the dogs. Rolly decided he might as well do a little investigative work while he was here, make his reason for visiting not quite so transparent.

"Hey, Joe, you know anything about the house that's down at the other end of the street?"

"Which one?"

"At the end of Starlight. Looks right over Black's." Rolly described the house.

"Oh yeah. They were having a party there last night."

"That's the one."

"Well, I don't know who lives there. Leslie might. I think maybe that's the one that used to be owned by that guy who ran off with everyone's money."

"Who?"

"I don't remember his name. This was about fifteen years ago. He had some sort of computer company. It turned out to be just a Ponzi scheme, though. A lot of folks in town invested money in the company. A couple of doctors I know up at Scripps lost their shirts."

"You don't remember his name? How about his company?"

"K-Tel or something? Nah. That was the company that made those greatest hits records you'd see on late-night TV commercials. I can't remember. I was back east in medical school at the time. Leslie told me about it when we were walking around the neighborhood one day."

"Hmm. Anything else?"

"That's all I know. You working some kind of case?"

"Maybe."

"You need me to report any suspicious activities?" Joe laughed. Even rich doctors liked to play gumshoe.

"Nah. Thanks. I'll see you later. Tell Leslie I stopped by. And have her call me if she remembers the name of the guy."

"You bet, Rolly. Give us a call. Come out for dinner sometime."

"Sure will."

Leslie was a great cook, but the thought of sharing dinner with both Leslie and Joe in their home was not all that appetizing. Rolly put the car back into gear and drove the rest of the way around the circular driveway, exited back on to the street. He was going to go home and lie down. He had to think this thing through before he went back to the mansion on the cliffs.

CHAPTER 11

▼

GUITAR BREAK

When Rolly pulled into his driveway, his mother stood in the garden, wearing gloves and holding a trowel. She wore her gardening smock—a long t-shirt printed with oversized sunflowers in yellow and black that was tied in a knot just at her knees. Doug and Will, the gay boys who shared the apartment next door, stood across from her. His mother laughed at something Doug said. Doug and Will laughed along with her.

Rolly got out of his car, waved at them, continued on into his house. He stopped on the porch, picked up his mail. There were a couple of bills and a copy of *Guitar Player* magazine with a white wrapper folded around it. Bold print on the wrapper warned him this was the last copy he would receive before his subscription was cancelled.

He threw the mail on the table, walked to the kitchen, and opened the freezer. He wanted something to eat. He hadn't slept much. His stomach rumbled. He had a lot on his mind. A pint of coffee ice cream or chocolate mint would be just the thing for it. But the freezer was empty.

He looked in the cabinet, found some saltines and peanut butter, grabbed a knife, and stood at the sink, snacking on crackers and Jiffy, drinking water from the kitchen faucet with a cupped hand. It was okay to be poor. He wished there was a way to get rich without getting himself into trouble.

He sifted through the events of the last twenty hours. This was a very different case than any he'd handled before. It was like reading a song chart without any melody, only the chords. There were a thousand combinations of notes you could use to connect them, but only one of them was the way the song had been written.

Rolly liked to think that solving cases was like writing songs. Most of his cases were simple blues tunes. You started with the basic structure. Somebody did somebody else wrong. That was the easy part. Cases like that started with the same bunch of notes, the same basic chords, but each client had their own special way of playing it. At least that's what it was like when you were dealing with missing husbands or wives, runaway teenagers. But this case was different. This one was more like a concerto, with an inviolable score written in tiny black notes. The orchestra had started playing before Rolly arrived. All he had was a triangle to play.

He took a last sip of water, wiped the knife clean, and put the peanut butter back on the shelf. The saltines were stale. He threw them away.

He walked into the bedroom and lay down on the bed. Getting excited, getting worked up was just the kind of thing that used to lead to drinking, then worse. It was important to keep his perspective on things, bring it all down a notch. He sat up, reached under the bed and pulled out the ES-335 guitar case. A little playing would be good for his mind. It allowed him to ruminate. Something about working through the chords, running a few riffs, helped him see more clearly, set his mind into order. Besides, the band had a gig at Patrick's tonight. He liked to spend a little time warming up before a gig, something he never would have considered when he was younger, more arrogant.

He cradled the guitar in his hands, felt the smooth wood, comfortable and familiar. He tossed off a few licks, bent the B string up a minor third. It twanged for a split second, then snapped, curling up around his right hand near the bridge. At least it had lasted through last night's performance. He put the guitar down, reached into the case, searching for a replacement. He popped open the small compartment in the middle of the case, sorted through the various strings in their paper envelopes, found one the right size. As he did so, he caught a glimpse of unfamiliar black plastic under the envelopes. His heart skipped a beat. He pulled out all the envelopes. There at the bottom of the compartment lay an item he had never seen before—a three-inch-long black plastic ellipse with a small metal extension at one end. It looked like the kind of gadget that might fit into the slots on the back of a computer. It fit the description that Ricky had given him. It looked like the Magic Key.

CHAPTER 12

▼

MARLEY'S LOFT

Marley Scratch lived in a loft on Broadway and Seventh Avenue downtown. He had long dreadlocks touched with a little shimmer of gold at the front edges. It was hard to say what he did for a living, a little bit of everything, as far as Rolly could tell—technical writer, concert promoter, web master, and reseller of vintage toys. He was also a respectable trombone player, and could pull a horn section together in a hurry if you needed one for a high-paying casual gig, the kind where they'd throw you an extra grand to bring along the horn section. Marley knew more about gadgets and mechanical things than anyone else Rolly knew.

Marley's loft covered the second floor of the Apex building. There wasn't much on the first floor anymore, a used bookstore, a greasy café, and the empty remains of Ace Music, at one time the largest music store in San Diego, where Rolly's father, at the insistence of Rolly's mother, had taken Rolly to buy his first electric guitar. Rolly had been twelve. It had been an infamous day in Waters family history, a kind of personal Pearl Harbor for all of them, the start of the war years.

To get in, you had to ring the doorbell on the west side of Seventh, wait for Marley to buzz you in, then walk up the fifteen steps to Marley's loft. It was a real loft, not like the new condos springing up like California poppies on the edges of the Gaslamp Quarter farther downtown. Marley's place was smelly, greasy, a little scary, with huge windows that started about eight feet off the floor and extended another eight feet to the ceiling. Rolly rang. Marley looked out from the window above. The door lock buzzed. Rolly walked up the steps.

"Maestro Waters, of the silver hands and leather heart." Marley bowed to Rolly at the door. "We are honored to welcome you."

Rolly wondered how old Marley really was. He could be thirty, he could be fifty. His skin was smooth and dark as a brand new Hershey bar, but the wrinkles on the skin at the edge of his eyes indicated at least a little hard time forcing a laugh onto a life's regrets. Hard to tell.

"What brings you here on a Sunday afternoon?" Marley asked.

Sunday afternoon at Marley's was always a ruckus of activity, filled with happy, screaming children of various hues. They chased each other around in the big open space, brandishing brightly-colored foam tubes as if they were broadswords. Some of them played video games on Marley's big screen TV. There were several women, as well, of varying ages and relations to the children. Rolly never asked whose kids were whose. Some were certainly Marley's. There were usually three or four guys gathered around some electronic gadget in back, taking it apart or putting it back together.

A tan-skinned boy with auburn hair, about six years old, ran up and hugged Rolly's leg, held on tight.

"Hey, little Rufus," said Marley,. "What'cha doing?"

Rufus smiled and peeked at Rolly from behind his leg.

"I've got something I need you to look at," Rolly said. "I think it's something for a computer. Is there someplace we can talk privately?"

Marley turned. "Follow me, Maestro. We'll go to my private domain."

Rolly followed. Rufus grabbed his hand and they walked along the brick wall to the far end of the room until they reached a large desktop, the size of a door, laid over two wooden sawhorses. A computer monitor and other pieces of electrical gear were strewn all about. Marley reached up, grabbed the edge of a gray curtain strung along a section of PVC pipe above them, pulled it closed. Rufus lost interest, let go of Rolly's hand and slipped out under the curtain.

"Whattya got for Marley today?"

Rolly pulled the plastic ellipse from his pocket, held it up in front of his face. "What is this?"

"That's a USB mini-disk for a computer. Where did you get it?"

"Someone gave it to me."

"I see. Who might this someone be?"

"I don't know. That's part of what I'm trying to figure out."

"Well," Marley began, "these are kind of new gadgets. They're not in the stores yet. I thought I had the only one in town. PC World sent it to me, asked me to test it, write a review."

"So it's something you could keep algorithms on?"

Marley laughed. "Algorithms? You been studying computer programming in your spare time?"

"But it is something you could store electronic files on?"

"Sure, algorithms, whatever. That's what it's for. Do you want to take a look at what's on there?"

Rolly handed the disk to Marley, who reached behind his computer and inserted it into a slot in the back.

"There it is," Marley said, pointing at the computer screen. Rolly followed Marley's finger. A small Eyebitz.com logo had appeared on the desktop. There was a long set of letters and numbers below it.

"Is that an algorithm?"

"No, no. That's just the name of the disk, maybe some internal tracking number from the factory. Let's take a look at what's on the disk."

Marley clicked twice on the disk icon and a window popped up. A list of numbered files appeared in the window. There was no apparent sequence to the numbers, but there was one file named "Start." Marley double clicked it. A message appeared on the screen: "Computer unknown. Encryption key not available."

"What does that mean?" Rolly said.

"It means the file is encrypted. It won't open unless I have the public key."

"What's that?"

"It's a digital key, basically a big, long number that's stored on the computer. When someone encrypts a file, only people who have that number can translate the file. If you don't have the number, you can't see the file."

"How do you get the number?"

"Well, usually, whoever gives you the file also gives you the number. He can give it out to whomever he wants. That's why it's called the public key. Once you have it you can read any encrypted files that person gives you."

"Can you open any of those other files?" Rolly said, pointing at the numbered file names. Marley clicked one. Another window popped up. This one was filled with a long set of numbers and letters in rows of pairs.

"Hex," said Marley.

"Hex?" repeated Rolly, wondering if Marley was talking voodoo.

"Yeah, hex code, that's what this is. It's programming code, the guts of a program."

"It's a computer program?"

"Yeah, or part of one."

"What does it do?"

"Hard to tell until you put it all together. This stuff is pretty meaningless unless you know what the program's designed to do."

"Could you figure it out?"

"I don't know. It would take me awhile. Where did you get this?"

Rolly considered his client's confidentiality for about two seconds. He needed to protect himself first, not Ricky or Fender or Curtis Vox.

"You've heard of Eyebitz.com?" he asked Marley.

"The guys with the video data stuff? What's this got to do with them?"

"They hired me to find this disk. At least I think this is what they hired me to find."

"You planning to give it back to them?"

"I haven't decided yet."

"Mmm, sounds like a dilemma. Do they know you have it?"

"No," Rolly lied. Somebody knew he had it. He just wasn't sure who it was. Rolly and Marley sat for a minute, thinking things through.

"Well," Marley said, "it's Sunday. How about if I take a look at this stuff tonight? You can have the disk back tomorrow."

"Thanks, I appreciate it."

Marley opened the curtain to the room. Rufus and the other kids were splashing their hands in the industrial-size sink that stood against the wall. Rolly heard the sound of pots and pans in the kitchen, smelled garlic and onions frying in olive oil.

"Want to stay for victuals?" Marley asked.

"Thanks, but I'm playing at Patrick's tonight. I need to get over there and set up."

"All right, I'll call you in the morning. Have a good gig."

Rolly walked down the stairs, got into his car and headed over to Patrick's. He could've stayed for dinner with Marley, but parking in the Gaslamp Quarter at night was a real pain these days, now that they'd made the place respectable, full of upscale restaurants and clothing boutiques. He hoped he could find a good parking spot before it got late, then grab a piece of pizza at Little Joe's with the guys, Bruce and Gordon, maybe Moogus. He wanted to lose himself in the familiar ritual of shooting the shit with the guys in the band, debating the merits of

Clapton and Cray and the Vaughn brothers, retelling stories of road-trip disasters and wild-woman encounters. And he wanted to commiserate with them for the ten-thousandth time about all the miserable musical hacks who'd made it big like they never would.

CHAPTER 13

▼

PATRICK'S CLUB

Sundays at Patrick's were relaxed. Easy. There was just enough of a crowd to keep things lively, but not enough of them drunk to ruin the vibe. It was a neighborly time of the week, mostly locals making the scene. Harry and Gina, the owners, were in recovery mode from the weekend craziness and couldn't be bothered with minor infractions. They weren't nearly as tight about managing things as they could be on Friday or Saturday.

Rolly liked playing at Patrick's. It felt like his own personal club. The room was small with a dark wooden bar that ran the length of the floor, a worn brass railing along the front of the bar, red leather stools. There were about a dozen small tables. Fifty people would fill up the room. From the stage the entire audience, the open front windows, and the street were visible. A lot of the patrons were regulars who came for the music, unlike most of the clubs in town. It was a real music joint, not just a place for trying to score with the opposite sex.

It had been a good night. The guys were playing well, paying attention. It was just after one in the morning. A modest crowd still remained as the band launched into the last number, Sam and Dave's "I Thank You." Halfway into it, Moogus started rattling the silverware, throwing all sorts of cymbals and syncopations into his beats. Rolly turned around to give him a disapproving look, saw Moogus staring out into the crowd with that ravenous look Rolly knew only too well. Moogus had spotted some woman who was making him stupid.

It was a drummer's disease, controllable but never cured. The best Rolly could figure was that a drummer was vulnerable because of his position on stage, sitting all night at his kit, hidden behind the rest of the band. All a drummer gets are quick glimpses of women down on the floor—a bare shoulder, a swish of blonde hair, a quick shot of cleavage. The women flash by like the girls in an MTV video, promising glimpses of erotic daydreams. Moogus handled his affliction worse than most. All through the set he'd be scouting the floor for the opposite sex, lining up targets. Then he'd get frustrated, start to lose focus. He'd start pushing the beat and throwing in all sorts of extraneous crap on the tom-toms and cymbals.

Moogus looked back, caught Rolly's eye. He shrugged his shoulders and laughed, settled back into the beat. Rolly turned back to the audience. Alesis was there. She was with Fender, at a table just off stage left. He hadn't seen them come in. Fender waved at him. Alesis gave an encouraging smile. Rolly started his solo. Alesis locked eyes with him. He let it go to his head.

Before long he was laying out every super-charged rock 'n' roll riff he could think of, pulling off the notes, trilling repetitive triplets, running way up the fret board. It was showoff, hackneyed, completely unoriginal, something he'd committed himself never to be anymore. Worse, it encouraged Moogus, who started throwing out all sorts of drum rolls on the tom-toms again. The audience ate it up.

Bruce and Gordon went along for the ride, but they tired out pretty quickly. Rolly saw them exchanging the look, the when-is-this-guy-going-to-get-over-himself sidelong glance that every guitar player has seen at least a hundred times in his life. They were ready to put an end to the evening, pack up their gear and go home.

Rolly made a dramatic gesture with his guitar and wound up the solo. The band finished the song with one of those big noisy endings that doesn't mean much, except that the evening is over. The audience applauded, let out a few yells, then headed for the front door. You don't get many encores on Sunday. The audience has to wake up in five hours and go back to work.

Gordon and Bruce left the stage, walked out back to take in the air and share a joint before packing up their equipment. Rolly kneeled down, grabbed a rag off his amp and wiped down his guitar strings, which were covered in sweat. Moogus stayed at his kit, breaking it down. He looked out at the crowd. He leaned his head down close to Rolly's.

"Ay yi yi, Rolly. Who's the talent sitting next to Fender? Don't tell me that's his girlfriend."

"Nah, I don't think so. They work together."

"Well, I've got something I'd like her to work on with me. Perhaps I'll have a visit with my dear old friend Fender."

Rolly looked over at Moogus, but didn't say anything. If Alesis was going to buy anything Moogus sold, she had a lot less on the ball than Rolly had come to think she did. Moogus put his snare in its case and unhooked his floor pedal. He crawled out from behind the rest of his kit, jumped down the steps, and bounced across the floor to where Alesis and Fender were sitting.

Rolly finished cleaning his guitar, placed it back in its case. He unplugged his amp, coiled up the cables, and put them into the guitar case. He stood up, turned back towards the room. Moogus had pulled up a stool next to Alesis. Fender looked up and waved. Rolly walked down the steps, picked up a club soda from Harry, and went over to join them. God, he was playing it cool.

"Hey there," he said as he reached the table.

"Hi Rolly," said Fender. "You're sounding great!"

"Hey there to you, rock 'n' roll star," said Alesis, turning away from her conversation with Moogus. The look in her eye suggested some sort of sincere appreciation. What sort, Rolly didn't quite know, but he was pretty sure it meant something good.

"Are you sure," Moogus said to Alesis, "that we haven't met before? You sure look familiar. Rolly, does she look familiar to you?"

"Oh, I think I'd remember if I'd met you before," Alesis said. She pulled out a cigarette and started to light it.

"You'd better not let Gina see that," Moogus said.

"What?"

"You can't smoke in any clubs now. It's the law," Rolly explained.

"Ah, shit. I forgot," Alesis responded. "I'd sure like a smoke."

"Well," Moogus chimed in, "if I can bogey a butt from you, I'll show you someplace you can smoke."

"Where would that be?"

"Out back, on the patio."

"I really need a smoke. You guys want to come out with us?" Alesis asked, looking back at Rolly and Fender.

Before Rolly could answer, Fender broke in. "You go on ahead. I've got something I need to talk to Rolly about."

"Don't go anywhere. We'll be back in a couple," Alesis said as she hopped off the bar stool. She tugged at the hem of her skirt. Moogus held out an arm to show her the way, making a big display of it. They walked up the stairs and disappeared into the hallway that led out to the back patio.

"So, Rolly, how's the case going?"

"I haven't had much time to get started. Probably tomorrow I'll get going."

"Did you talk to Curtis yet?"

"Not yet."

"He's hard to get hold of, I guess."

Gordon and Bruce returned from their smoke, which meant Moogus had Alesis all to himself out on the patio. Rolly resisted the urge to go check on them.

"Hey, Rolly!" someone shouted. It was Gina, waving him over from her table by the front door. She counted out a stack of money. When Gina called with the cash, you had to obey.

Rolly excused himself, walked over to collect.

"Friend of yours?" Gina said, glancing over Rolly's shoulder towards Fender.

"Yeah, an old friend."

"Who's his girlfriend?"

"I don't think she's his girlfriend."

"So I guess you got a chance, then."

"You keeping an eye on me?"

"I got to watch out for my boys."

She counted out two hundred dollars, tossed in two twenties for tip.

"There you go. Don't spend it all on one woman."

"What I really want is a chance with you, Gina."

Gina laughed. She loved to flirt with the guys in the bands. It kept Harry from taking his good luck for granted. Rolly walked back to Fender, who was talking on his cell phone. He turned it off as Rolly arrived.

"Hey, Rolly," he said. "I need a favor."

"What is it?"

"Can you give Alesis a ride home? I have to go meet with King."

"At one-thirty in the morning you have to go to work?" Rolly regretted the question. He was more than happy to give Alesis a ride.

"King says it's really important."

"That was him on the phone?"

"Yeah. He keeps kind of weird hours. I don't think he sleeps."

"Sure, I can give her a ride."

"Thanks, Rolly. It will really be a big help." Fender stood up, as obsequious as ever, then stuck out his hand to shake Rolly's, as if they were making a deal. Rolly shook. Fender pulled out his car keys.

"Have fun," Fender said, and walked out the door.

Rolly watched Fender leave. Bruce and Gordon had packed up their gear and cleared out. At the end of a gig they were always on time. Moogus' drum set was still up on stage, disassembled, but not yet packed up in its cases.

Moogus always said that Sunday night was the best night to get lucky because the next day was Monday. The woman would have to leave early to get ready for work. And if she didn't leave early, you could pretend that you had to go to work. There was no pretext of hanging around. A woman who was out late on Sunday wasn't looking for love. She was out to get laid.

Rolly sat at the table and finished his soda. He wondered if it was true.

CHAPTER 14

▼

A MOOGING

Alesis walked back down the stairs and over to Rolly.

"Where's Fender?" she said.

"He had to go to work. King called him."

"He called him at this hour? Jesus, he's such an asshole."

"I said I could give you a ride."

"Oh, you did, huh?"

"Where's Moogus?"

"He went to get his car. There was a parking spot open in front of the club."

An open parking spot in front of the club was golden for drummers. Even for Moogus, it was more important than sex.

Alesis sat down, put her chin in her hand and looked at him sleepily.

"You know, you're pretty handy with that guitar," she said. "I could have used you in my group."

"What was the name of your band?"

"The Chiclets. It was an all-girl band."

"I don't look very good in a dress."

"You could have played on the record. We had some guys play on the record."

"You made a record?"

"Yeah, an EP."

Every band Rolly knew made an EP back in the eighties. They all wore skinny ties on the cover. The new wave/punk thing. Everyone and their brother (or sister) had a self-produced Extended Play record. It was more than a single, less than an album. If you sold a couple thousand copies the record labels might show an interest in you.

"Is that when you went to Japan?" Rolly asked.

"Yeah."

"How was that?"

"The first night was great. We had a big crowd. After that it was kind of a mess."

"What happened?"

"Someone died." Alesis stared off into the corner of the room, as if suddenly taken with the quality of the woodwork.

"Someone in the band?"

"Hmm?"

"Who died?"

"Oh. Our backer. The guy who put up the money."

"What happened to him?"

Alesis snapped back into focus, looked at Rolly again.

"He just died. That's all. We had to cancel the tour."

"So how'd you wind up working at Eyebitz?"

"I know King."

"Oh, right. You used to go out with him?"

"A long time ago."

"Well, I guess you still get along."

"Let's just say we understand each other."

"He asked you to work for him?"

"That was my idea. I told him he had to hire me."

"What do you mean?"

"Nothing. He owed me. That's all."

Rolly was silent. Alesis' mood had soured a little.

"Well, it's getting late. I guess we better get going," he said.

He walked back up to the stage and hauled down his gear. They said good-night to Gina, who unlocked the front door and let them out. They walked past the Crab Shak restaurant next door. Rolly nodded at a waiter, who was standing outside, smoking a cigarette. The waiter glanced down at Rolly's guitar case.

"Hey, you with the band?" the waiter asked. He tilted his head in the direction of Patrick's.

"Yep," Rolly replied, expecting a musical critique. Everyone has an opinion at two in the morning.

"Come with me. There's a guy inside, says he's with the band. Somebody mugged him."

Rolly and Alesis followed the waiter inside. The late-shift bartenders and waitresses were cleaning up, refilling the ketchup bottles, rolling silverware up in cloth napkins. In the corner of the room, back towards the kitchen, near the door to the patio, a small group gathered around a man seated in a wooden chair. The man leaned back in his chair, holding a large white towel over his face. One of the waitresses knelt down beside him with a glass of ice water.

"Moogus?" Rolly said.

Moogus pulled the towel down from around his eyes, leaving it bunched up against his nose. The towel was red with blood. Alesis gasped.

"What happened?" Rolly asked.

"Some guy jumped me, man. I was going to pick up my car. This big guy walks up to me. He was six-foot-six, at least. He just walked up to me and slammed me. Shit, I don't know. It happened so fast."

"Did he say anything?"

"Yeah. He said, 'I'd like to inquire as to the whereabouts of the key.' Then he kicked me a couple of times while I was down."

Rolly turned to the waitress.

"Have you got any aspirin or something?" He took the glass of water from her. She walked back to the kitchen to look for some.

"Moogus, who was this guy? Have you ever seen him before?"

"No. It all happened so fast. He just stood there for a couple of seconds blocking my way. He smiled at me like he knew me, just stood there looking straight at me in his Hawaiian shirt and puka shells. He said, 'I'd like to inquire as to the whereabouts of the key.' I said 'How would I know where your freaking keys are?' Then out of nowhere he decks me."

Rolly glanced at Alesis, wondering if she was thinking the same thing he was. She looked a little sick.

"Do you want to call the police?"

"We already called them," said the waitress, returning with a couple of pills.

"Can we please move to the back patio?" said another employee, approaching them. "We need to get the floor mopped."

Rolly, Alesis, and Moogus moved to the back patio, where Moogus and Alesis had gone for their smoke. It was an old brick courtyard shared by the rear exits of the Crab Shak, Patrick's, and Croce's around the opposite corner. The back windows of an old brick apartment house looked down from above. There were iron chairs and a table, a small decorative fountain. It was a nice little spot, except for the stink of old crab shells floating up from the dumpster. Alesis shivered.

"Here, take my jacket," said Rolly. "It's a little sweaty, but it'll be warmer than what you've got on."

"Ooh, rock star sweat," Alesis said, wrinkling her nose, but taking the jacket.

"I think I'd better wait here until the cops show up. Do you want me to call you a cab?" Rolly offered.

"Pretty expensive cab ride to North County," she shrugged. "I'll wait."

Rolly thought about offering to split the fare with her, decided against it. The night was probably shot, but he'd still like some more time with her, alone.

Moogus leaned forward in his chair, looked at Alesis over the top of his towel.

"You know, I still think I know you from somewhere," he said to her. "Are you sure you never dated a drummer?"

"I don't think so. No drummers in my past. A couple of guitar players maybe." She winked at Rolly.

"Guitar players, huh? Well, you should try dating a drummer sometime."

"Is that a proposal?"

"You see, guitar players can only play with two hands. Drummers can coordinate all their extremities." Moogus was incorrigible. Even with blood dripping from his nose and a dark welt puffing up around one eye, he was hustling her.

"Hey, Alesis," Moogus said, "how does a guitar player change a light bulb?"

"I don't know."

"He holds it up and the world revolves around him."

Alesis laughed, looked over at Rolly. "Are you gonna take that?"

Moogus seemed to feel better than he looked. If he wanted war, he could have it, at least until the police showed up.

"Oh, I can beat that," said Rolly. "Why is a drum machine better than a drummer?"

Alesis shrugged.

"Because it can keep a steady beat and won't sleep with your girlfriend."

She laughed.

"What do you call a drummer who breaks up with his girlfriend?"

"You're killing me, man," Moogus moaned.

"Hey, you started it."

"What do you call him?" Alesis asked.

"Homeless," Rolly replied.

There was a noise from inside the Crab Shak and a policeman entered the courtyard. A paramedic followed behind like his shadow.

"Is the victim here?"

Moogus raised his hand.

"That's me, officer. I'm the victim. Thank God you're here to rescue me from this offensive jokester."

The paramedic knelt down beside Moogus, pulled the towel back to take a look. The officer spoke to Rolly and Alesis, got their version of the story before turning back to Moogus.

"Hey, kids," Moogus said, waving at Rolly and Alesis, "go home. I'm all right. I don't want to spoil your fun."

Rolly glanced at the paramedic, who unwrapped some gauze from his kit.

"I think he'll be okay," said the paramedic. "I don't think it's broken. We'll check him into the emergency room for an x-ray to make sure. They'll probably just send him home with some Percoset."

"Okay," said Rolly, torn between leaving Moogus and getting Alesis out of there. "I'll tell Gina you're leaving your gear overnight. I can pick it up for you tomorrow."

"Rolly, you know something really weird?"

"What?"

"After the guy hit me, I was lying on the ground. He was walking away, and I heard a harmonica playing. I can't believe it. I got my ass kicked by some dumb-ass harmonica player."

CHAPTER 15

▼

ROLLY'S HOUSE

Rolly and Alesis left the Crab Shak and walked back to Patrick's, knocked on the door. Rolly told Gina about the drums. He didn't tell her anything more. She would have wanted to hear the whole story. She would have gone into a long speech about how dangerous it was getting downtown, how it wasn't a neighborhood anymore. Rolly didn't have any more time left in him to listen.

They headed back east on E street, across the intersection at Fifth. Rolly pulled the cart with his amp and guitar along with his right hand. Alesis walked next to him on his left. As they reached the opposite corner, Alesis reached out her hand and slipped it under his arm, getting close.

"That was kind of scary," she said.

Rolly was scared, too. "It comes with the territory," he said.

"What do you mean?" she said.

"Oh, you know, the late nights, playing in bars. It's not the safest environment."

"Anyone ever hit you?"

"Oh yeah, a couple of times," he lied. It was, perhaps, the most remarkable thing about his whole bar-playing, whisky-drinking, girl-chasing career. He'd never once taken a punch. Not from a bar patron, a jealous boyfriend, or a pissed-off band member who'd spent one too many nights on the road in roach-infested motels with him. Not once. Rolly had always been able to talk his way out of anything, even drunk. He'd smile and start talking. He'd back away slowly. Taking a punch was what drummers were for. Like Moogus tonight.

"Here we are," Rolly said as they arrived at his Volvo. He opened the passenger door for Alesis, stashed his amp and guitar in the back seat. They'd have to make room for a woman tonight. He climbed into the driver side seat, flipped the key in the ignition, and looked over at Alesis. The sulfur-yellow light from the street lamp above reflected a small glint of moisture in her eyes.

"Are you okay?" he asked. She tried to smile, but didn't get far, half sleepy, half sad. She looked hopelessly sexy.

"We've met before, you know," she said.

"What do you mean?"

"Me and you. We met at a party. Your band was playing. Back in the eighties."

"Really?"

"Yeah, we did. You don't remember me, do you?"

"If I'd met you before, I think I would remember."

"I had my band then. Everyone at the party said I should meet you. They said you were going to be a star. There was an article in the newspaper about local bands, 'Most Likely to Succeed,' I think it was called. You and your band were on the list."

"Yeah, I remember that."

"At the party, I kept trying to talk to you, but your girlfriend was jumping in all the time. She kept dragging you away whenever I tried to be friendly."

"How friendly were you trying to be?"

Alesis smiled. "I made friends with your singer. What was his name?"

"Matt?"

"Yeah, that was it. He doesn't play with you anymore?"

"He's dead."

"Oh shit. I'm sorry. When did that happen?"

"About five years ago. He was in a car accident."

"I'm sorry."

They were silent for a moment. Rolly had her sympathy now. He might as well test it.

"You want to come home with me?"

Alesis stared at him, unresisting. It was like watching a balance tip up and down inside her head.

He started backtracking, trying to rationalize it for her. "It's been a weird night and it's an awfully long drive to North County." Even saying it, he didn't know what he wanted. He was either the smoothest operator or the nicest guy in the world, maybe both. She'd been sending him signals all night. He felt pretty sure of that. But seeing Moogus had left them both a little unsettled.

"You're a nice guy," Alesis said. "Let's go."

Rolly turned the ignition and pulled away from the curb.

When they got to his house, he cut the lights before entering the driveway. If there was one thing he didn't want now, it was to wake up his mother. He pulled his equipment from the back of the car and they walked toward the house. It had taken eight minutes to drive to his house from downtown. Alesis had stared out the window for all but thirty seconds of it.

"Here it is," Rolly said. He opened the door and turned on the light. The room looked awfully bare. There was nothing like bringing a woman home to reveal how pitiful your living conditions really were, even if she didn't say anything. It all became clear the second she entered the room. You could see it all with her eyes.

"Geez, look at all these guitars," said Alesis. "Do you really play all of them?"

Rolly closed the door, leaned the guitar case against the dining table.

"Oh, sure. I play all of them. Some of the time." He was nervous. He tried to remember the last time there'd been a woman inside his house. A woman who wasn't his mother. He couldn't remember. Leslie had never been here.

He waved his hand toward the bedroom. "That's the bedroom in there. You can have the bed if you want and I'll take the sofa." Why was he pretending he didn't want her? He was old, out of practice, losing his touch.

Alesis turned and stepped close, her silk blouse brushing against him. He looked into her eyes. She was taking him in like a dark lonely tunnel on a steep mountain drive. She'd made a decision. He was glad someone had.

CHAPTER 16

▼

WAKE-UP CALL

Rolly's eyes blinked open. Sunlight drilled into his head. It must be late. He reached over and pulled the alarm clock closer so he could read it. Ten-thirty exactly. He turned back over to look for Alesis, but she wasn't there. He lifted his head, listening to see if she was still in the house, maybe in the bathroom or, God forbid, trying to make breakfast. He didn't hear anything. He dropped his head back onto the pillow, stared at the ceiling, happily re-running last night in his head.

When they got to bed, Rolly figured they were in for a cuddle, maybe one of those slow, sympathetic little screws where both partners stay quiet, even at the end. But pretty soon, Alesis had turned it into something wilder. She came out of her sad little shell screaming like a stack of Hiwatt amps cranked up to ten, begging him to pick all her strings, run up the frets, and slam down the whammy bar. It was the kind of sex he wanted every night when he was twenty-one, never imagining he would prefer any other variety. Of course, when he was younger, all those acrobatics didn't make him sore in the thighs, in his butt. It didn't leave him unable to stand up straight because his lower back was so stiff.

"You're one hell of a fuck for such a nice guy," she whispered to him, her head on his shoulder, stroking his stomach afterwards. She was funny. "One hell of a fuck for such a nice guy." He couldn't get over thinking he'd heard that before. Then he fell asleep.

He opened his eyes. There didn't appear to be any further adventures forthcoming, so he got up, crumpled the discarded condom wrapper that was on the nightstand and threw it in the trash. Alesis was a well-prepared woman. He put on a t-shirt and shorts and walked out to the living room. The guitar case from last night leaned against the wall by the phone. He thought he'd left it against the table. It had been late. He couldn't remember. For once, he'd been thinking about something besides his guitar.

There was a note on the table, written in pencil on the back of an Ernie Ball guitar strings envelope.

"Decided to call a cab, after all. Had to go to work. Thanks for taking care of me. You're a nice guy."

Well, at least she'd left a note. He reread it for clues, measured the tone, took it to mean he had half a chance for another round if he wanted to follow up.

The phone rang. He picked up the receiver.

"You're one hell of a fuck for such a nice guy."

The voice was deep, nasal, definitely not female. Rolly almost jumped out of his shorts.

"What?"

"One hell of a fuck for such a nice guy." There was a big laugh at the other end of the line. He couldn't mistake that voice, even with its newly plugged, nasal tone.

"Moogus, what the hell's going on?"

"Aren't you going to ask how I'm feeling?"

Rolly flashed back to the scene at the Crab Shak, Moogus absorbed in his bloody towel with the policeman and paramedic beside him.

"Hey. Sorry. How are you doing?"

"I'm doped up on Vicodin and feeling fine. I've developed a lovely mix of dark green and purple around my left eye, but I'm pleased to report that my nose is only slightly damaged and my handsome profile should remain unblemished. Thanks for asking. Hey, how's your girlfriend?"

"She's not my girlfriend."

"You sleeping with her?"

"No," Rolly lied. Having Moogus know anything about your sex life was only providing him with ammunition for later needling.

"Well, you should. I remembered where I know her from."

"Where?"

"You remember that recording session we did about fifteen years ago for that movie?"

"What movie?"

"New Wave Nudes. You remember?"

Rolly didn't remember, but he knew Moogus was going to help him. And he had the distinct feeling it wasn't going to be all that fond a remembrance. They rarely were.

"That porn flick. Your lady friend was the star. That's how I remembered. That line, it cracked me up: 'You're one hell of a fuck for such a nice guy.' That's what she says to this guy at the end. It's like the last line of the movie. I knew she looked familiar. I've still got the videotape. I checked it out when I got home last night. She's got this blonde, moussed-up eighties hair-do and she's twenty years old, tops, but it's definitely her. It's a very impressive performance. I give her four stars for fornication."

Rolly's head was swirling. He didn't know what Moogus was talking about, but it raised an icky swell in his stomach. He needed some coffee.

"You don't know what I'm talking about, do you?" said Moogus. "All those years of sex, drugs, and rock 'n' roll have just completely screwed up your memory, haven't they?"

"Hmm?"

"Okay, let me take you through it again, slowly. This is like fifteen, sixteen years ago. That whole punk/new wave thing is happening and everybody in town has got a band. You and me and Bruce were living down in Ocean Beach, The P-15s, playing every frickin' bar in town, five six nights a week. We weren't making a dime though, 'cause whatever we made went right back up our noses."

"Yeah, we had that one bedroom near the boardwalk."

"Yeah, okay, now you're on it. So we played this party in Point Loma. Big place, with the view out to Coronado and downtown?"

Rolly imagined he could remember it. He'd played a lot of parties in big houses with views of the city. He couldn't expect to remember them all.

"And this guy starts talking to us, tells us he's producing a movie, says he wants to hire us to play on the soundtrack. We're not really buying it, but the next day he calls us, tells us to come by Mixed Up next week, bring our equipment and just do some jamming. He says he'll throw us five hundred bucks for a couple of hours work."

Rolly began to see a picture in his mind, still too dim to determine if it was real or just something he'd created from Moogus' description.

"So we get there," Moogus continued, "and they've got this video monitor set up to show us the movie. The guy from the party is there. He gives us a check for five hundred bucks. Of course, that asshole J.V. Sideman's there to toot his lame-ass riffs. He's always around when there's easy money to be made." J.V. Sideman played saxophone with every blues band in town. Moogus hated Sideman. Sideman hated Moogus. Their feud was legendary amongst local musicians.

"So they set up the recording gear, we do a little sound check, and then they start the movie. And it's this cheesy suck and fuck flick. There's some kind of plot about these girls starting a band, but they have to blow all these guys to get a record contract or something."

Rolly sat down at the table now, rubbing his head. The memory was hazy, but definitely real. He could picture the session, but not the movie.

"Anyway, it's definitely her. I've got the videotape if you want to see it. You can decide for yourself if your girlfriend there is worth pursuing."

Moogus was having the time of his life. He started back into his usual rant about J.V. Sideman. Rolly let him roll, tuned him out, started running new thoughts around in his head.

He wasn't all that upset about Alesis and the porn flick, if it really was her. She had things in her past she wasn't proud of. So did he. Maybe that's why they'd hit it off. That line bugged him though: "Pretty good fuck for a nice guy." Maybe it was just a little joke she couldn't even remember where she got anymore. But thinking about it, he started to feel there had been something just slightly scripted about it, about the whole evening. He felt another twinge in his gut. He stared at the wall next to the table, his guitar case leaning up against it. He was pretty sure that when they'd come home last night he'd put it against the table. It had moved.

He listened to Moogus, let him wind down. It was only polite. Moogus had taken a punch for Rolly last night, although Moogus didn't know it. The least Rolly could do in return was let Moogus keep talking until he was finished.

"All right, buddy," Moogus said, "I gotta go pick up my drums. I'll see you next week."

Rolly hung up the phone. He reached out, pulled his guitar case over to him, held it for a second, then set it on the table and popped the latches. He pulled out the Stratocaster and strummed a few chords, fiddled with the pegs until the tuning was right. He started singing,

> *There was a man, called Hercules*
> *He had the kind of muscle, he could do just what he pleased.*
> *But even he was not exempt*
> *He had to clean the stable where a thousand cattle slept.*

CHAPTER 17

▼

ITEM OF INTEREST

The phone rang again. Rolly answered.

"Hey, Rolly. It's Marley."

"Hey. You get anything?"

"Not much. I don't think I can do anything else without that encryption key. There was one file I was able to open. It's an mpeg."

"M peg?"

"Yeah, digitized video. Some scene from a sex movie."

Rolly leaned his arm on the table, held up his head.

"Rolly?"

"Yeah."

"Whattya want me to do? You want the disk back?"

"No, hang on to it. I've got a couple of things I need to figure out. I'll call you back when I need it."

Rolly hung up the phone, sat silent for a moment, wondering just how full of coincidences twenty-four consecutive hours could be. His stomach tweaked like crazy. He looked at the clock. It was eleven-thirty. He wanted to call Alesis, listen to her voice, find out if the tone of it would tell him anything. But he didn't call her.

He needed breakfast, something substantial to chew on. A *machaca* plate from the taco stand began calling his name. He walked to the bedroom, threw on a pair of jeans. He put on his loafers, no socks, grabbed his wallet and headed out the front door. As he left the porch, he picked up the newspaper and tucked it under his arm. Maybe reading a few box scores would clear his head, a glance through the headlines. The rest of the world was in a lot worse condition than he was. He hoped so, anyway.

He headed over to Robinson, turned onto Fourth, walked up to the corner of Washington where the taco shop stood with its pastel-green slanted roof. It had a bright yellow sign with red lettering on it that spelled out "La Posta."

The sun was out, warm, not quite hot. Rolly picked up his order, sat down at one of the concrete tables that fronted the shop along Washington. He tore off a piece of flour tortilla, dropped a couple of forkfuls of *machaca* into it, folded it over, and bolted it down. A little grease dripped from the corner of his mouth. He wiped at it with a napkin, took a sip from his Coke. His stomach felt better. He could start to think clearly now.

Whoever it was that had attacked Moogus had somehow confused him with Rolly. Perhaps they had seen Moogus at the party on Saturday night, carrying Rolly's guitar case. It didn't matter. Someone was willing to get rough in order to get at the disk. It was only a matter of time before they came after Rolly.

As for the video Marley found on the disk, it could be the same one Alesis was in, but it probably had nothing to do with the case. If Alesis had been in the movie, she no doubt had fans, Moogus among them. Curtis Vox might be a fan, as well. Maybe Curtis liked to carry dirty pictures of her around on his high-tech key chain, thrilled to know that a woman he worked with was a porn star. Rolly hoped it was something that plain and simple. Sometimes sex was just sex. But why had Alesis moved his guitar case?

It was time to stop playing big-time detective, time to accept his limitations and act rationally. He was in over his head. He'd pick the disk up from Marley today, mail it back to Eyebitz.com, no return address. Ricky and King Gibson would be satisfied. They wouldn't ask questions. Fender would telephone Rolly to inform him that Eyebitz.com no longer required his services. Rolly could fill in his blank check for five hundred dollars and call it a day. He didn't want to hear any more about Magic Keys, secret algorithms, or exploding computers. He didn't care any more about options or money. He didn't want to see any of these people ever again. He just wanted out.

He finished his meal, sipped the last of his soda, and watched the world on Washington Street pass around him. He liked watching people, taking in the small pieces of lives they played out in public, listening to the delicate second-line rhythms that fill in the spaces between the day-to-day beat of the city. He felt better now that he'd made a decision.

It was noon. Nurses and interns from the hospital across the street stopped by in their scrub gear to catch a quick bite, taking a break from twelve-hour shifts. Two gay men in matching white tank tops, khaki shorts, and sunglasses trotted up to the window, ordered bean and cheese burritos with a side of sliced carrots and chilies. A teenaged girl stood at the bus stop, dressed in an oversized pair of blue jeans, gray t-shirt, and navy-blue watch cap. She wore a small silver stud in her nose. Her left ear was pierced with six different pieces of metal. Rolly counted them all.

He opened the paper, checked the Padres score first. They'd lost again, three to two in ten innings. Things didn't look good for a pennant run. He scanned through the world news. There were five-and-a-half months left until the end of the twentieth century, at which point computers all over the world were going to explode. At least that's what it sounded like.

He moved on to the Metro section. Construction on the new baseball park was going to be held up again while various citizens sued the city. One of those suing the city this time was Max Gemeinhardt, Rolly's lawyer. Max had purchased season tickets since the team's very first year in the majors, but he was dead set against taxpayer spending for corporate robber barons. At least that's how Max described it. Max was always suing some arm of government, be it city, state, or federal. He'd actually beaten the IRS once when they tried to nail him for tax evasion. He sued them back, made them cry uncle. When it was all over, the IRS ended up sending Max a check for two hundred thousand dollars.

Max had been Rolly's lawyer for the last five years, ever since the accident. He hadn't charged Rolly a dime in that time. Max's hobbies were birding and baseball. He used to listen to rock 'n' roll bands and chase women, but at seventy-two, he'd retired from both those pursuits. He had three ex-wives, ten million dollars, and a house built of glass on the beach in Del Mar. He didn't think much of anyone else who had money.

Rolly started reading again. A headline in the lower right corner of the page caught his eye. He read it again. The headline said, "Body found at Black's Beach."

CHAPTER 18

▼

BODY MOVES

Rolly read it again: "Body found at Black's Beach."

A body found at Black's Beach was identified yesterday as that of Curtis Vox, chief technology officer at Eyebitz.com and a former student at UCSD. Authorities have yet to determine a cause of death, although the detective at the scene suggested that Vox may have fallen from the notoriously unstable cliffs above. Police at the scene observed torn clothing, some scratches and cuts on the body. When reached for comment, Eyebitz.com CEO Ricky Rogers said, "We are shocked and saddened to hear this news. Curtis was a friend, a great talent and a key part of the Eyebitz.com team. He will be impossible to replace."

Mitch Ibanez, a former professor of Mr. Vox at UCSD, describes Vox as a student of great potential and promise. Police reported receiving an anonymous phone call early Saturday morning requesting a patrol car at the house where Vox lived, but no one answered at the residence when the patrolman arrived. An Eyebitz.com company party had taken place at the home the previous evening.

There was a picture of Curtis Vox. It wasn't much of a picture, the one notable feature being the long black hair cascading down either side of a bland, androgynous face. It was the same man Rolly had seen floating in the pool Saturday night.

He looked up from his paper. The sun was still out, but the small steady rhythms of the street life around him had given way to an insistent loud pulse in his head. He read the article again from the start. Found dead at Black's, that's what it said. Which meant Curtis Vox had traveled a couple hundred feet to the west and down a steep cliff sometime after becoming a corpse.

The sun was unbearably hot as it glared down on Rolly's head. A large bead of sweat dripped down the left side of his face, slid down in front of his ear. Ten minutes ago, he'd had a solution. This had all been about corporate trade secrets, maybe a woman's embarrassing past. Now dead bodies were moving around. Between the time Rolly had left the house in The Farms on Sunday morning and the time police arrived there, someone had dragged Curtis' body from the pool to the edge of the cliff. That someone could have been there when Rolly went back to pick up his guitar. That someone knew that Rolly had been there. And that someone knew for certain that Curtis Vox didn't die from a fall off a cliff.

Rolly stood up, cleared the table, started walking towards home. He felt exposed, unprotected. The world he'd been watching was now watching him. It was like that bad dream he used to have all the time, the one where the band started a song and he would play out of tune, unable to figure out what key they were in while the band members, the audience all glared at him, disgust and disappointment all over their faces.

When he got back to the house, he sat down at the table, read through the article again just to seal it. He pulled out the business card Ricky had given him, dialed Ricky's number. The line rang twice. Someone answered. Alesis.

"Mr. Roger's office."

"This is Rolly."

"Did you hear? Isn't it terrible?"

He felt relieved. There was shock in her voice, that sound you can't hide when someone you know is suddenly gone. She might be guilty of something, but she didn't know anything about this.

"Yeah, that's why I called. I wanted to talk to Ricky."

"He's in a meeting now, all of top management. They're discussing what we should do."

"About Curtis?"

"Well, yes, about the company. Curtis was a really important person to us."

"Yeah, I heard." He wondered if she had any idea how important Curtis was to him personally right now.

"Well, just tell Ricky I called."

"Rolly?"

"Yeah."

"Last night … do you think what happened last night had anything to do with this?"

"You mean Moogus?"

"Yes."

"Why would I think that?"

"I just wondered. He said the guy was asking him about a key."

"What do you think that has to do with Curtis?"

"It's just all these things happening at once—Curtis losing the key, Moogus, and now Curtis dead."

"Maybe, I don't know. Just have Ricky call me when he gets a chance."

"Rolly?"

"Yeah."

"I'm sorry."

"Sorry about what?"

"About last night, I mean this morning."

"I had a good time. Let's leave it at that."

"Yeah, me too. There's just a lot going on I need to think about. Sorry, I gotta go."

"Bye."

"Bye."

He hung up the phone. He didn't want this kind of trouble, whatever it was. Playing private detective was just a day job, a way to keep busy and bring in a couple of bucks. Why couldn't his life ever be simple? All he wanted to do was make enough money to spend the rest of his time playing guitar, keeping his chops up, performing a few nights a week.

He looked around at the guitars in the living room, the sunburst Telecaster, the gold-top Les Paul, the sea-foam green Epiphone, each one displayed in its own special spot. Each one was a woman with a ticklish soul. Each one had a story to tell. He waited for one of his beautiful harem to start talking to him. The Martin Dreadnought caught his eye, with its blonde spruce top and big woody curves. It suckered him in with its abalone eyelets and dark, resonant mouth. He pulled out a bottleneck slide and picked up the guitar. He sat on the sofa and started playing.

He picked out some blues notes, played sad chords with minor sevenths, the only things he could ever depend on. When he was fourteen, he would hide in his room playing guitar, turning the headphones up loud so he could drown out the sound of his father and mother, the bitter and angry sounds that they made as they fought a war out in the kitchen. He'd keep on playing until he fell asleep with the old Esquire wrapped in his arms.

He settled into a little groove with the acoustic, ran through "Come on in My Kitchen" and "Crossroads." He improvised on a riff in B, found a set of chords he liked, and played through them a few times, listening, hearing them a little differently each time. He thought about Alesis, about a secret computer disk, and a dead kid in a swimming pool. He thought about the shadows that were following him.

Right after the accident, he'd given it up, stopped playing entirely, sold every instrument that he owned. He didn't trust it, couldn't separate the music from all of the crazy things that seemed to go with it, the late nights, the ego battles, the dishonest club owners and booking agents, the drugs and alcohol, the easy, unhappy women.

But he had returned to it, little by little. One day his mother brought home a guitar, something she'd paid fifty dollars for at a garage sale. It was the Gibson ES-335 and it looked as beat up and worn out as he did. He didn't play it at first; there were no strings. He tried to imagine how it would sound, how it would feel. Then he started repairing it, replacing the truss rod and the tuning pegs, cleaning and polishing. He bought some strings and a case. He let himself play it, fifteen minutes a day. Then he'd put it in the closet, testing himself, making sure that the devil inside him wouldn't escape from its cage. He collected old records— T-Bone Walker, Tampa Red, Elmore James. He listened to each note they played, the spaces between them, beautiful things he started hearing again in a new way. He played the guitar a little more each month, learning to listen instead of just play, beginning to hear the beautiful things that were inside him, as well.

He played through the set of chords, running the riff again, repeating it over and over. There was a song in it somewhere, but he didn't have all the notes yet to connect it together. A lyric popped into his head, something he'd seen on a book cover. He sang it quietly, a little phrase that fit in with chords.

> *This is the soul of a new machine.*
> *This is the soul of a new machine.*
> *This is the soul of a new machine.*

CHAPTER 19

▼

THE PROFESSOR

Rolly found himself on the freeway again, driving north on Interstate 5 along Mission Bay, past Pacific Beach and into the heart of the fault line along Rose Canyon. He was spending a lot of time on Torrey Pines Mesa lately. He pulled off at Genesee Drive and drove up to the UCSD parking kiosk.

"Can you tell me where Wagner Hall is?" he asked the parking attendant.

The attendant pulled out a map, drew a winding path in yellow magic marker, took Rolly's money, and slapped a permit on the Volvo's windshield. Rolly pulled into the parking lot, climbed out of the car, and headed in the indicated direction towards Wagner Hall.

He was there to see Mitch Ibanez, the professor quoted in the newspaper article, the one who praised Curtis Vox as a student. While playing his guitar, Rolly had decided he needed more information on Curtis, a different perspective than the one he had heard from Ricky, from Fender and Alesis. Curtis was a genius, but an odd duck, that was the company party line. He was also the man who had last been in possession of the Magic Key. Rolly wanted to hear about Curtis from someone unconnected to Eyebitz.com.

He called UCSD information, got the professor's phone number. Then he called the professor's office, got an answering machine. He left a message introducing himself as Detective Waters, asked the professor to call him back. He waited about fifteen minutes before he got antsy. The message on the machine listed the professor's office hours—noon to two on Mondays and Thursdays. It was one o'clock when Rolly called. If Professor Ibanez was in his office, Rolly might be able to drive up to the university and catch him before he left. As he entered the building, he glanced at his watch. It was almost two. He walked up the stairs in quick steps, waited and caught his breath at the top before proceeding.

Wagner Hall Room 302 was small, filled with books and papers from floor to ceiling. A somewhat round, middle-aged man sat behind a desk, looking distracted. He wore reading spectacles, which hung on the end of his nose by the thinnest layer of skin cells imaginable.

"Professor Ibanez?"

"Mmm?" Ibanez replied, not looking up from his work.

"I'd like to talk to you."

"My office hours are from noon until two." The professor looked at his watch, then back at his papers. "It is now 2:04. Office hours are over."

"I called earlier … about Mr. Vox."

Professor Ibanez looked up from his papers, assessing Rolly. "Are you the detective?"

"Yes, sir. Roland Waters," said Rolly, offering his hand. Ibanez remained seated, motioned Rolly to the industrial strength green plastic chair in front of the desk.

"You don't look like a detective, Mr. Waters."

"What does a detective look like?"

"Well, I have spent most of my morning talking to several of them. I was just beginning to define a simple heuristic regarding their appearance and manners. I shall have to see if this new rule of thumb needs to be reformulated or if you are just an anomaly. Is there a particular reason the police keep sending people out to talk with me?"

"I'm not with the police."

"Oh … you did say you were a detective, did you not?"

"Yes, sir. I'm a private detective. I was hired by Eyebitz.com."

"Well, that might explain the difference in appearance and manners. Has the company hired you to investigate Curtis' death?"

"No. I was hired to investigate another matter related to Mr. Vox."

"Do you think this matter has something to do with his death?"

"Not that I'm aware of. From what I know, Mr. Vox fell off a cliff when the ground gave way under him. The police say it was an accident."

"Yes, that's what I was told. Well, what did you want to ask me?"

"I just wanted your take on Curtis Vox."

"My take?"

"Well, what was he like? You seemed to think pretty highly of him in the paper …'a student of great potential and promise,' I think you said."

"Yes, I might have said that. Curtis was very intelligent."

"It's kind of what you didn't say that I was interested in," Rolly said. Playing guitar, back in the house, he had thought about how the space between the notes was sometimes as important as the notes you actually play.

"What I didn't say?"

"Well, the words you used—'potential,' 'promise.' What do you mean by that? Was he a good student?"

Professor Ibanez leaned back in his chair, pulled his reading glasses from his nose and clicked the two ends together thoughtfully for a moment.

"An astute question, Mr. Waters. To answer it directly, I would have to say no. Curtis was not a good student. In fact, as I recall, I gave him a C in my course."

"But you said he was intelligent."

"Extremely. He could have been an excellent student. He chose not to be. He had a hard time managing the requirements for regular class attendance and completion of assignments. He seemed to find it more worth his time to devise ingenious computational tricks of dubious value."

"Like what?"

"Well, he created a program that appeared to delete all of a user's directory on the lab workstations. It would run the first time a user deleted a file, which made the user think they had done it themselves. It didn't really do any damage, but he managed to scare several students. Some complained."

"Anything else?"

"Well, he inserted an item into one of my lectures."

"What kind of item?"

"A scene from a pornographic video."

That's the beginning of a pattern, at least, Rolly thought.

"I'm not absolutely certain it was Curtis," the professor continued. "I caught the item before I started the lecture and deleted it. Curtis seemed the most likely suspect, though."

"Could you describe the video?"

"Excuse me?"

"I was just wondering if there was anything in particular you noticed about the video."

Professor Ibanez glared at Rolly. "I didn't really watch it once I found out what it was."

Rolly decided to change the subject.

"Did Curtis have any friends, any romances?"

"None that I know of."

"None at all?"

"You probably know the stereotype of computer programmers, Mr. Waters."

"You mean that they're nerds?"

"Yes, nerds, dweebs, geeks. It is something of a myth that computer programmers lack social skills, but there are enough around that do to remind you where the stereotype comes from. Let's just say that Curtis was not the first student we've had in the department who lacked social skills."

"In what way?"

"Curtis seemed to have an inborn need to prove he was smarter, or at least more of a smartass, than anyone else. He had a bad habit of taunting other people when they couldn't keep up with him."

"How so?"

"If someone made a mistake, he'd make fun of him, tell everyone how stupid he'd been. It became harder and harder for Curtis to attract people to work with him. At first, students wanted to work with him because they knew he was smart and could help them do better. After the first year or two, the other students avoided him like a plague."

"When did he graduate?"

"He never graduated. He quit, to work for Eyebitz.com, just before starting his senior year. That was about a year ago."

"What can you tell me about Eyebitz.com?"

"What would you like to know?"

Rolly was beginning to feel that Professor Ibanez was a man who didn't like open-ended questions. "Well, I mean, what is it? Do they really have some sort of revolutionary technology like it says in the brochure, some kinds of new algorithms?"

"Well, I don't really know much about the company. I've heard the buzz and the rumors, but that's all I've heard. They seem to be playing it pretty close to the vest with their product."

"You mean they're hiding something?"

"I'm not saying that. But they have yet to roll out a real product. They've never allowed anyone to go over it, kick the tires, so to speak."

"From what I understand, they're worried about industrial spying, back door engineering."

"Backward engineering, I think you mean," said the professor. "Well, yes, I suppose that's a legitimate concern, but until you have a product people can use, it's all vaporware, anyway. That's how it is these days, in this business environment. A kid like Curtis gets a good idea, works up a couple of algorithms, next thing you know someone's tossing him ten million dollars in venture capital. Pretty soon everybody else is worried they're going to miss the next Netscape or Apple Computer and more money starts pouring in."

"You don't seem to think they've got much of a product."

"I'm not saying that, either. I'm just saying I don't know what they've got and there's no way *to* know until I see something that's not held together with baling wire and band aids."

"Meaning?"

"The demo versions of the software they've released are clearly built on open source technology that's already out there. You can tell if you poke around in it a little bit. They've licensed it and tweaked it a little, but that's all it is. Nothing revolutionary. On the other hand, maybe the technology doesn't matter if you know how to sell it. Don't listen to me if you want investment advice. I put all my money on a company called Kaydell back in the eighties."

"They didn't do well?"

"Oh, they did worse than that. The CEO absconded with all of the investors' money."

Rolly nodded sympathetically. Was that a Kaydell party he'd played in Del Mar way back in the eighties? It was some kind of computer business everyone was excited about. They had a big cake at the party, shaped like a computer. Rolly got drunk at the party. He tripped, fell, put out his hands to break the fall, and stuck them into the cake. The guys in the band made him stay in the parking lot the rest of the night, when he wasn't on stage.

Rolly sat for a moment, waiting to see if Professor Ibanez wanted to volunteer any more information, but there was nothing forthcoming. He stood up, pulled a business card out of his wallet.

"Thank you, Professor Ibanez. If you think of anything else that might be useful, please give me a call."

CHAPTER 20

▼

THE WATERFRONT BAR

Officer Bonnie Hammond of the San Diego Police Department sat at her regular window table at the Waterfront Bar, nursing a Corona, her once-a-week indulgence and reward for sticking to her six-day-a-week workout schedule. She was out of uniform, wearing a blue plaid Madras shirt that matched her eyes. She wore Doc Marten boots and black Levis. In the late afternoon sun her blonde tomboy haircut reflected a few red highlights that matched her freckles. She was five-foot-six, 170 pounds, and built like a Chargers cornerback, lean, mean, and speedy.

The Waterfront was a dive in Little Italy (Microscopic Italy, some in town joked) that had managed to survive its age and decay to become popular with people the regulars would have abhorred in its more blue-collar days. Where once it had been the exclusive enclave of tuna fishermen and the longshoreman's union, it was a more motley crowd that frequented the place now. Salty sea dogs were being squeezed out by well appointed urban professionals, lawyers, accountants, and the India Street arts crowd, dressed up in tattoos and attitude.

Tangerine-colored townhouses were under construction on either side of, and over, the bar. A dozen Italian restaurants had sprung up in the neighborhood where there used to be two. You couldn't walk half a block in the neighborhood anymore without running into an espresso machine.

Bonnie was a creature of habit and self-enforced routine, as dependable as anyone Rolly had ever known. Every Monday for the last ten years she'd been at the

Waterfront Bar at five-thirty in the evening, celebrating the start of her police officer's weekend by sitting at a window table and sipping on a *cerveza*. The new crowd didn't bother her. It was the only time Rolly ever saw her drink alcohol, even when she used to stop by to cruise Joan, the sound tech at the Bacchanal Club. Bonnie had pretended she came to hear Rolly's band, but he always knew what she'd really been after.

Rolly didn't have many friends in the police department. None, really, except for Bonnie. He'd never felt comfortable around policemen. He didn't know any musicians who did. They were preternatural enemies, musicians and cops, as far as Rolly could tell, complete opposites in temperament, personality, style. Cops were dedicated to order. They had to control their emotions to do their job well. Musicians made their living from exposing their emotions in front of others.

"Hey, Rolly!" Bonnie called as he walked down the sidewalk.

"Bonnie!" he said, delaying a little, faking surprise, pretending his mind had been somewhere else. He walked over to her, hopped up on a barstool across the table from her.

"Can I buy you a club soda?" she asked.

Bonnie knew Rolly's history. Rolly suspected Joan had told her all about it. And Bonnie had found him drunk once in a deserted doorway on K Street downtown at four in the morning. She'd taken him home. She could have put him in jail.

"With a lime." Rolly smiled.

"With a lime," repeated Bonnie, motioning the waitress over and ordering.

"How's Joan?" Rolly asked.

"She's good. We're good, if that's what you're asking. You gotta stop by and see the house sometime. We just finished the kitchen—all new appliances, floors, and fixtures. It's looking sweet."

"You're going to make a lot of money on that place," Rolly said. Bonnie and Joan were fixing up a Victorian in Golden Hills, an up and down neighborhood to the east of downtown. But you couldn't go wrong anywhere in this city buying real estate.

"Yeah, but we don't want to sell yet. We want to enjoy it a little. So what are you up to? Still chasing down whiny teenagers for their unhappy mommies?"

Bonnie's friendship had survived Rolly's transition to private detective, but she didn't think much of his second profession.

"Yeah, same old stuff—gigging a couple nights a week, picking up a case here and there. Nothing too exciting. Just helping some folks out. Which is how I like it these days."

He wanted to broach the subject of Curtis Vox, find out if any rumors might be floating around the station. Cops couldn't keep quiet if something was hot. He'd bide his time, though. He didn't want Bonnie thinking he was after anything yet. He'd drop it in naturally, if he could.

The waitress dropped off his club soda, glanced at Bonnie's beer which was still three quarters full. Bonnie was a cocktail waitresses' nightmare. She stayed at her table forever and sipped her drinks slow. She was a cop at the end of her week and she didn't give a damn what the waitress thought.

"You still in touch with Leslie?" Bonnie asked. She and Joan had gotten together while Rolly and Leslie were still a couple. They had even double-dated a couple of times.

"Haven't talked to her much. She got married a couple of years ago, you know. Lives in La Jolla, nice house in The Farms."

"Yeah, I heard that. Have you met the husband?"

"Yeah. He's a doctor. Nice enough guy."

"Any regrets?"

"She's better off with him."

"You're not carrying the torch?"

"It wouldn't do me any good if I were. He bought her a nice old house right near the road down to Black's. She can drop down to the beach anytime she wants."

"She'll want to be careful about dropping down to the beach around there."

"Hmm?"

"Just a joke. Some guy fell off the cliffs the other night."

Rolly's attention picked up. This was the chance to move the conversation into his territory.

"Some Zonie trying to get down to see the naked bodies?" Zonie was the locals code name for anyone from Arizona, but it could be used to refer to any half-witted tourist from east of the county line.

"No, it was a local, some kind of computer programmer. He was living up there. Twenty-one years old and he's got a whole mansion to himself on the cliffs. I'm in the wrong business."

"I could have told you that."

"Yeah, like you should talk. Or are you getting rich sometime soon?"

His Eyebitz.com options popped into his head. Why hadn't he just returned the key when he first had a chance? It was time to drop Bonnie another bit of information.

"I might be. I started working for an Internet company last week."

"No shit, doing what?"

"Oh, security stuff, consulting on corporate espionage," he said, pumping things up just a little. "It's a company called Eyebitz.com."

"Yeah? That's the place where this guy was working."

"Really? What's his name?"

"Curtis Vox."

"I don't think I've met him. So what did he do, just walk off a cliff?"

"Nobody's sure what happened. The cliff might have given way. He had a key to get through the gate down to the beach, so he didn't need to climb down. It was night. The fog was pretty thick. It seems unlikely he was standing there just to look at the scenery."

"Well, I'll tell you one thing, the employees are wound up pretty tight at this place. Maybe he just couldn't handle the pressure."

"The coroner hasn't ruled out suicide." Bonnie looked at Rolly. "The thing that bugs me is I was at the guy's house the night before."

"What for?" Rolly said. This was a stroke of luck.

"A phone call came in, anonymous, said there was a dead body in the pool. I'm working La Jolla night shift last weekend so I got the call. I went up, but I couldn't find anything. Nobody answered the door. I could see the swimming pool, but no one was in it."

"And this guy shows up dead the next day? That sounds suspicious."

"Don't start getting any ideas there, buddy," Bonnie said. "You let the real detectives handle this one."

Bonnie was a good cop. She'd been close to something and had missed it. Rolly knew that it bothered her. He knew that Bonnie couldn't help feeling she could have done something to prevent Curtis' death.

"My lips are sealed," Rolly said. It was time to change topics. He could sneak back around to it later.

"Somebody beat up Moogus on Sunday night," he volunteered.

"What?"

"Yeah, outside Patrick's. Some guy just walked up to him on the street and decked him."

"Is he okay? You filed a police report, right?"

"He got a bloody nose and black eye, but he's back to being himself. An officer and paramedic came down, checked him out. I'm sure there's a report somewhere."

"Man, that pisses me off." Bonnie didn't like Moogus. She thought he was an overbearing, sexist jerk. And Moogus had slept with Joan once, during a time when Bonnie and Joan weren't getting along. But Bonnie didn't like anyone getting beat up on her streets, especially someone she knew. She took it personally.

Rolly drained the last of his soda, sucked the juice out of the lime wedge. "Well, he'll live, anyway. I gotta get going." He took out a business card, handed it to Bonnie. "I'd like to see the house sometime. Give me a call."

"See you later," said Bonnie. "I'll let you know if we find out anything about the guy who hit Moogus."

Rolly left the bar and walked back to his car. He might call Bonnie later, tell her more about Eyebitz.com. He might be able to suggest a connection between the mugging of Moogus and her case. She might drop him a little more information on Curtis Vox. Friendships were always worth something.

He stopped at the taco stand on his way home, picked up some rolled tacos and a *carne asada* burrito. He should eat better, start buying some food at the grocery store. It would make his mother happy if he lost a little weight. He promised himself he'd start buying groceries next week.

He walked into the house, dropped the bag with his dinner onto the table, and checked the phone machine. The first message was from Max, inviting him to the Padres game that night. It was enticing, but Rolly wanted to stay home for the evening. He'd call Max tomorrow, pretend he hadn't picked up the message in time, which wasn't a complete lie. There was only about a half hour until game time.

The second message was from Fender.

"Hey, Rolly," Fender said. "Ricky wants you to be at our board meeting tomorrow morning. La Jolla Shores Beach parking lot at 7:30. Bring a bathing suit."

CHAPTER 21

▼

BOARD MEETING

At seven o'clock Tuesday morning Rolly joined the weekday commuters. He crawled north on Interstate 5, stuck in his Volvo wagon, cursing the other drivers around him. The weather was drizzly and gray, imperfect, the kind of photo the Visitors Bureau liked to keep out of travel brochures.

He had on the only pair of swim trunks he owned, as bright and lime green as the day Leslie purchased them. Leslie believed in the beach, as if it were some kind of all-purpose therapy. Rolly hated the beach, the strange smells in the air, the sweaty, half-naked crowds that littered the sand on hot summer weekends. The swim trunks had gone straight to the bottom drawer of his dresser, stayed there untouched by sunlight or surf.

The trunks were uncomfortable, tight at the waist, stretched to their limits around his thighs. He'd called Fender twice last night, but got no return call. What kind of board meeting did you have at the beach? He shifted his butt in the driver's seat, wondered what the hell he was doing.

He took the Ardath Road exit, about a mile south of Genesee, sat in traffic for what seemed like an hour. He took a right on La Jolla Shores Drive, drove down a few blocks, then left into the beach parking lot. The last time he could remember being at the beach this early in the morning was when he was sleeping one off after a gig in Ocean Beach. He'd walked around all night trying to find the apartment he'd just moved into with Moogus and Bruce, but he'd been too drunk to find his way home. He lay down on the sand against the boardwalk and went to sleep. When he'd woken, arms wrapped around his guitar case, his clothes had been covered in vomit and sand, his head pounding in pain.

The Shores parking lot was quiet, shrouded in mist. He parked the Volvo, got out. He shivered as he closed the door. A few early striders were taking their morning constitutional along the concrete boardwalk. In the grassy section just to the north of the lot, he saw a group of people huddled together. He headed towards them.

As he moved closer, he heard someone making a speech. The speaker was Ricky. Twenty or so Eyebitz.com employees stood in a circle around Ricky, like apostles in warm-ups and wetsuits. Surfboards were stacked at the edge of the circle like loaves of bread, wetsuits like rubbery fish. Rolly looked for Fender, then for Alesis, but he didn't see either one. He stopped a few feet outside of the circle and listened to Ricky's sermon.

"We have lost an important piece of our team," Ricky said. His voice was soft, modulated, suggesting deep seriousness. "We can take this loss, allow it to hurt us, or we can use it to make us stronger." Ricky paused, caught Rolly's eye for just a split second.

"We are all riding a wave," he continued. "And some of us will fall off the wave. Some of us will get back on our boards and some of us won't. And once in a great while, one of us may drown. That is the chance we take. Every day. The wave is stronger, the ocean bigger than any of us. We can't fight it. But we can ride it. The key to our thinking, our business, is not to fight the wave, but to become one with it, using its power, anticipating its movement. We surf it together. We use our eyes, our ears, our hands, our feet, and our minds, all working together. If we get cautious, if we lean too far back, we miss the opportunity, we lose the real power of the wave. If we press too hard, we get underneath it. The wave overtakes us, drops down on top of us. It grinds us into the sand."

Ricky turned as he talked to the crowd, looking directly into their eyes, addressing each employee personally. They hung on every word, swallowed them down like margaritas on a Saturday night in Tijuana. Ricky might be talking about surfing, but he meant business, religion, and life. Rolly watched Ricky's face as he spoke, saw the focus, the mania, the evangelical look in his eye.

"There is no perfect wave," Ricky continued. "There is only the wave you are riding right now. We've caught our wave. Our challenge now is to ride it for as long as we can, to adapt as it changes form and shape. We'll drop down the face, slide through the curl, and hang on through the chop. We can't look ahead to the shore. We can't look back to see if a bigger, better wave is behind us. This one is ours. Don't fight it. Be one with the wave. We don't have the power to change it.

But we do have the power to stay with the wave, to ride it out wherever it goes. Stay with the wave."

Rolly wondered how you could be riding a wave at the same time you were anticipating it, but decided not to worry about it. You weren't supposed to understand what Ricky said. You were just supposed to go with it. Like the wave.

Rolly was still half asleep, but the Eyebitz.com employees were ready to go. They had their affirmation now, their consolation, their pep talk. They burst at their seams with that go-get-'em vibe that he'd seen before in timeshare salesmen or EST graduates. Rolly thought about Leslie, about the Reverend Terry Cole Whitaker sessions she'd forced him to attend every Sunday at the old El Cortez Hotel ballroom downtown. Ricky emanated the same kind of vibe.

"Let's ride," Ricky crowed. There was a brisk flash of action as the congregation dispersed, picked up their surfboards, and headed out towards the waves. Some of them wore wetsuits with an Eyebitz.com logo inscribed above the left breast.

"Mr. Waters, welcome. Do you surf?" Ricky said, moving towards Rolly.

"Not in a long time."

"Well, today's as good a day as any to start again."

"Fender told me you wanted to see me?"

"We'll talk business out on the water. Put on a wetsuit and grab a board. I would love to re-introduce you to the power of the wave," he enthused. "I'll meet you out there."

Ricky picked up a surfboard, attacked the beach at a canter, overtaking the trailing members of his flock. Rolly stood alone on the grass, amidst a jumbled pile of discarded clothes, Eyebitz.com branded wetsuits, and surfboards. He sighed, took off his shoes and shirt, squeezed into one of the wetsuits. He'd been through a lot in his life. He'd seen a lot of weird things. But this was one of the weirdest. He lifted a surfboard and strode out towards the ocean.

He was ten years old the last time he'd been on a surfboard. It was the day his father had left on a six-month tour of duty off the Vietnam coast. Rolly and his mother drove to the beach at Coronado, a white stretch of sand flanked by the old Hotel Del and the North Island Naval Air Station. They watched his father's destroyer pass out of the harbor. It sailed past the Point Loma lighthouse and soon disappeared over the horizon.

There had been a big fight the night before, his mother and father yelling at each other downstairs. The morning after had been full of silences, ending in unsure embraces.

After the destroyer passed out of sight, Rolly picked up his surfboard and paddled out into the ocean. The wave sets were flat. He bobbed in the water, pulled
at a piece of kelp, waited for something to ride. He saw a small brown lump floating towards him. As it got closer he realized it was a human turd, bobbing on the
surface. The ocean was just a big toilet, as contaminated as the rest of his life. His
parents were flushing their marriage away and his life along with it. They were
toxic and Rolly was too. He sat on the board, watched the turd drift away, then
paddled back into shore. It was the last time he'd ever been surfing.

So here he was twenty-nine years later, still feeling poisonous half the time,
shivering with the first cold splash inside his wetsuit. He had to paddle his ass off
just to get out past the first line of breakers. A big spray of white water hit his
board. He gagged on a mouthful of salty slime. First rule he should have remembered—keep your mouth shut.

But his persistence paid off. He made it out past the breakers and turned back
around, facing halfway to shore. He'd managed to pass a few floundering Eye-
bitz.com employees on his way out, but it had cost him. He wheezed, trying to
recapture oxygen. He was tired and cold. It was hard to understand why people
enjoyed this.

He sat up on the board, tried to maintain his balance, moving his legs wildly
in the water around him. The board shifted back and forth under his butt. Ricky
waved at him from twenty feet off to the right. He wondered if Ricky was calling
him over, but before he could move, Ricky had turned his board towards the
beach and caught the next wave coming in. Ricky was a good surfer. He finished
his ride, hopped off the board. He turned around and paddled back in Rolly's
direction. Someone joined him, a large man who bulged through his wet suit as if
it might burst at the seams. The wetsuit was wrapped so tightly around him that
even a few drops of water were unlikely to slip inside of it.

As Rolly sat on the board waiting for Ricky, he kept shifting his feet, still
working to maintain his tenuous balance. He finally managed to spread both legs
way out on either side of the board and find a semi-comfortable equilibrium.

"You made it," Ricky said, as he pulled up on Rolly's right.

Rolly looked out to sea, felt relieved there were no promising waves on the
horizon, turned back to Ricky.

"Fender said something about a board meeting?"

"This is it," Ricky said, tapping lightly with his fingers on the board between
his legs. "Surfboards. Every Wednesday for any employee who wants to come
out. It's a little teambuilding exercise I put together. On my orders, the company

bought two-dozen boards, wetsuits, and a trailer to carry them in. Walter here is responsible for taking care of them."

He indicated the larger man, who had taken a spot about six feet off Rolly's left. It was the same man who'd been practicing yoga in his office, the one who played the harmonica. Up close he had a vague, empty look in his eyes. He rested a pair of massive knuckles on the board under him, turning them over ever so slightly like a silverback gorilla.

"Mr. Waters, is there any reason you might be unhappy with our business arrangement?" asked Ricky. Walter grunted low under his breath. He appeared to be smirking, if it was possible for an ape in a wetsuit to smirk.

Rolly waited a moment, as if he were thinking, which he was, but not about his business arrangement with Ricky. He recalled the recent arrangement of Moogus' face and wondered if Walter worked in the face arrangement business when he wasn't hauling surfboards or holding the lotus position.

"No," he said. "I'm perfectly happy with our arrangement. Why do you ask?"

"I haven't had any communication from you. Did you contact Curtis? Have you had any conversation with him?"

"Curtis Vox is dead."

"I'm aware of Curtis' death, Mr. Waters. I have discussed it with my employees, news reporters, and police detectives. I have not slept for the last thirty-six hours because Curtis Vox is dead. My question for you is did you have any contact with him before he died?"

"No. I did not."

"You were aware that it was he who originally reported the Magic Key missing? We did discuss this in our meeting on Sunday, did we not?"

"Yes," Rolly said.

"Then I'm curious as to why you did not contact Curtis. It seems to me that would have been the place to start."

"I was unable to contact him," Rolly said. "I went to the house. I tried calling him too."

He was telling little lies. They didn't matter. Curtis was dead before Rolly had even been hired. Someone had placed the Magic Key in Rolly's guitar case at the party, the night before his visit to Eyebitz.com headquarters. Had Curtis put it in there? Did anyone else know about it? Did Ricky?

"Mr. Waters, I sincerely believe that some of the smartest, hardest-working people in the world work for me here at Eyebitz.com. They expect to be well rewarded for their talent and efforts," Ricky said. He spread his arms out expansively as if to claim the group of people bobbing on the waves in front of him. He was king of his people, the big Hawaiian. His subjects ran naked and free in the sun. They were building a shiny new money machine for him, paving the way to riches and fame.

"Yes, I'm sure they do," Rolly said. He looked at the surfers, watched as the smartest, hardest-working, soon-to-be well rewarded employees of Eyebitz.com tried to stand up on their boards, lost their balance, tumbled into the water in various ungraceful ways.

"You will be well rewarded, also, Mr. Waters, if you find and return the Magic Key. I think we've made that quite clear."

"Yes," Rolly said. His surfboard drifted towards Walter's. The big ape was silent, gazing towards shore.

"I expect a lot from the people who work for me, including you."

"I understand," Rolly said. His outstretched left foot had drifted within inches of Walter's surfboard. He pulled it back underneath his own board, which was a mistake. The surfboard tipped to the left.

He fell into the water. It was cold and nasty, a briny wet in his nostrils. His wetsuit provided buoyancy, though, and he floated back towards the surface. But his head bumped against something solid, preventing him from breaking through. His path was blocked. He panicked, started thrashing his arms. A muscular leg was in front of him, the flat underside of a surfboard against his head. A large hand reached down, made its way towards him like a five-legged octopus. He turned his face, trying to get away from the hand. It grabbed the back of his neck, held tight for a couple of seconds, then pulled him back to the surface.

Rolly gasped for air, looked into the eyes of Little Walter, who lifted him up like a wet kitten.

"Be careful," Walter said, releasing his grip. "The ocean is beautiful, but it is treacherous." His voice was high-pitched, raspy, as if halfway through puberty it had stuck in his throat.

Rolly said nothing. He turned away and remounted his surfboard.

"I'm glad we had this talk, Mr. Waters," Ricky continued as if nothing had happened. He turned his head, looked back at the ocean.

"Here comes a good set," Ricky said as he flattened himself on his board and paddled away hard. Walter did the same, heading off in the other direction. Ricky looked back at Rolly and pointed.

"Start digging, Mr. Waters! The next wave's for you."

Rolly pressed himself down on his board, pointed towards shore and began stroking the water. He had to get back into the beach somehow. This way was as good as any.

CHAPTER 22

▼

THE SEAWALL

Rolly floated into the shallows, hopped off his surfboard, stood up. He wiggled his toes in the sand. It was good to be back on solid land, away from the nervous feeling he got sitting out on the water with only an unbalanced piece of resin and foam between himself and the ocean below.

As he walked across the sand towards the boardwalk, he heard a loud, angry voice. Ricky stood on the beach by the seawall, holding a cell phone up to his ear. Fender stood next to him, on the other side of the wall, dressed in a homely brown suit. He looked as uncomfortable as Rolly had been out on the water.

"Listen, my friend," Ricky screamed into the phone. His left hand pressed against his temple, as if to keep his head from exploding. "Listen, my friend, if I don't have those numbers on my desk by noon, heads will roll. I want to review it today. Believe me, if I don't have signoff on this today, heads will roll. Heads will roll."

Ricky snapped the phone shut, pointed towards Fender. He lowered his voice, stabbed Fender several times in the chest with his finger. Rolly couldn't hear what he was saying.

A ringing tone played off to Rolly's right, someone's cell phone or a pager. It was playing the intro to "Stairway to Heaven." Another ring went off to his left. "Fur Elise" was the tune of choice this time. Two more phones started ringing farther away. Eyebitz.com employees began scrambling, ran in from the waves or sat up on the sand. They opened their towels, dug in discarded trousers and shoes, pulled out cell phones and punched at the buttons. The wrath of Ricky buzzed and beeped its way through the invisible network of wireless nodes. Rolly could almost trace the path of accountability and blame from cell phone to cell phone, beach towel to beach towel.

Ricky left Fender and headed back to the parking lot, flipping his phone open again as it started ringing. Rolly walked over towards Fender, sat down on the wall.

"What's that all about?" Rolly asked.

"Oh, nothing," Fender replied. "Just some stuff Ricky wanted. He's got a presentation on Friday for a group of investment bankers."

"Seems to have caused quite a commotion."

"Ricky gets people going."

"Puts the fear of God in them?"

"I guess so," Fender said. "It's worth it, though. Look at what happened to Yahoo!, to eBay, Amazon. All of the people that started those companies are going to be millionaires."

"Hmm," Rolly nodded. The beach was almost deserted now. People rushed back to their cars, dumping their wetsuits and surfboards in a pile on the grass, still frantically talking on phones as they climbed into BMWs, Jeeps, and Miatas, and screeched out of the parking lot.

"How long do people have to put up with Ricky before they get rich?"

"The IPO is next month. We've got some cheap, locked-in shares we can sell the first day if it goes well. The real money will come in if we stick around for another year or two."

"I guess that keeps people pretty nervous about getting fired?"

"Yeah."

"So nobody's rich yet?"

"No, except maybe for Ricky and King. They're rich from before. They'll just be richer."

"Yeah, I read about Ricky's last business. What does this King Gibson guy do?"

"He's like an investor. He advises Ricky on financial stuff. He's providing the money that helps keep us going until we go public."

"He expects to get his money back, I assume?"

"He expects to get it back ten or twenty times over. He's what's called a 'phase-one investor.' He doesn't have to wait for a year before he cashes in all his shares."

Rolly paused. It sounded like King Gibson had a pretty good deal.

"What about Curtis?"

"Curtis was going to make a lot of money too."

"He wasn't rich already?"

"No."

"So how could he afford to live in that house?"

"Oh, King set that up."

"King owns the house?"

"He knows somebody that does. He's got connections."

"I guess King just wanted to show his appreciation to Curtis, huh?"

"Yeah," Fender said. He put his hand to his forehead, smoothed out his brows. "That was part of it."

"What was the other part?"

Fender rubbed his chest where Ricky had poked with his finger.

"Rolly," he said, "you can't tell anyone else about this, okay?"

"Sure," Rolly said.

"Curtis was kind of weird, you know, different."

"Different, how so?"

"Well, he was kind of free in his attitude, his lifestyle. It bothered some of the other people at the office."

"Free, how?"

"Well, um ..." Fender looked down at his shoes. "He liked to work in the nude. He said it helped him think clearly when he was coding."

"Coding?"

"You know, programming the computers."

"I guess I'd call that a little weird."

"He usually worked late at night, so it wasn't a problem. There weren't that many people around. He had this robe he'd throw on if someone knocked on the door. But at some point he didn't care anymore. He'd walk down the halls or show up at meetings without his clothes on. People complained."

"So Mr. Gibson politely offered to put him up at the house?"

"Yeah, that's what I heard, at least."

Rolly considered the information Fender had given him. It was one more layer of weirdness, but it did make a kind of sense.

Someone started playing a harmonica. Rolly glanced around for the source. Walter sat on the sand about fifty feet away, his back propped up against the seawall. He was the one playing the harp.

"What about Walter, there?" Rolly said, nodding his head in Walter's direction.

"Little Walter?"

"Little Walter? That's his name? Like *the* Little Walter?"

"I dunno. Who's that?"

"Great Chicago blues harp player. A lot better than this guy."

"Well, that's just his nickname. I don't know where the name comes from. That's what Curtis called him."

"I guess it's supposed to be some kind of joke because he's so big. What does Walter do?"

"He's director of maintenance."

"Maintenance of what?"

"Oh, the building, security, maybe. I don't really know. King brought him in."

Rolly listened as Walter tortured the harp. Rolly wanted to walk over, look Walter straight in the eye, and tell him his harmonica playing sucked. He wanted to act like the drunks that hid in the corners of the nightclubs he played, timing their half-shouted insults for maximum impact. He wanted to stuff the harmonica down Walter's throat.

But he didn't. It was time to do a little research. It was time to leave the beach and start hitting the stacks.

CHAPTER 23

▼

THE LIBRARY

The public library downtown was a utilitarian block of rectangular concrete, built in the 1960s. It rejected all sunlight from its three-story, tan exterior walls. The insides were frayed at the edges, with busted toilets, fallen ceiling tiles, and dry, musty stacks, attended by brave, listless librarians marking time nobly while waiting for the day when city leaders might find the courage to spend money again.

It was a tired old shrine to the public good. Rolly loved it. It looked like he felt, unkempt and underappreciated, but deep inside it, if you worked hard enough, you could find knowledge and wisdom. Rolly had spent three years of his life here, and down at City Hall, doing research for Max and his lawsuits. It was because of the time he'd spent here that he'd been able to qualify for his investigator's license. You had to have three thousand hours in the state of California. It had all happened because of the accident. The job Max had given him to keep him out of jail had turned into months and then into years, three thousand hours of poring through ownership deeds and microfilm and phone books, looking for names and addresses and dates. When Max retired, Rolly couldn't imagine working for anyone else. He decided to get a license, start his own business.

Before going to the library, Rolly stopped by City Hall, the Office of Records, looked up the ownership deeds for 1186 Starlight Drive—the address listed on the crumpled photocopy of the party invitation he carried in his pocket. Two owners were listed. The most recent, G. Tesch, had bought the house in 1985.

The man he bought the house from was Anthony Kaydell, as in Kaydell Computer, the company Professor Ibanez regretted investing in.

Which was why Rolly was now at the library, reading through old newspaper stories on Kaydell Computer, tracing the path of its notorious founder through the tiny news lines burned into microfilm.

Kaydell promised to create computers for the masses, underselling the competition by almost 50 percent. He did it by underselling his own costs by at least 30 percent. The company lost two hundred dollars every time it sold a computer. But no one knew that. Investors bought into the vision. The money piled up. Kaydell joined the social set, made friends in the city council, donated thousands to the mayor's re-election campaign. He supported the arts and financed an alcohol-free rock 'n' roll club for teenagers. Everyone felt fortunate to have a man of such vision and talent making himself part of the city's bright future.

Then Kaydell bought a sailboat, made an announcement. He was selling his house in The Farms and sailing solo around the world. He planned to return with a new vision for the next great paradigm in the computer business, along with a plan to make it all happen. His boat was found at sea three days after he left, abandoned and empty. His body was never recovered. Mexican pirates were blamed.

Soon thereafter the Kaydell Company unraveled. Before leaving on his voyage, Kaydell had apparently raided the company coffers, transferring large sums of money to an offshore account. There was nowhere to go for a company that was losing money on every computer it sold. There never had been. Investors sued, but there weren't any assets to claim. There weren't any Mexican pirates either, just an ingenious con man who'd made an exquisite exit.

There was a photo of Kaydell. He had a large, fuzzy mustache and shag haircut, which, even at the time, had been out of date. Rolly wondered if all con men were fashion impaired. All the ones he'd encountered were behind the times in their choices of clothing and hair. Perhaps it helped in the con, made the marks feel slightly superior, luring them into believing the con man was an eccentric genius who couldn't be bothered with the latest styles.

Rolly printed the page with the picture. He folded it up and slipped it into the back pocket of his pants. He left the library, walked to his car, and drove home.

When he walked into the house, there was a message on his phone machine.

"Mr. Waters, this is King Gibson. I have some things I wish to discuss with you, information I think you might find useful. I'm at the Hyatt Aventine in La Jolla. Please join me for dinner at six."

There was a game being played at the management level of Eyebitz.com, first Ricky and now King wanting to talk to him. But who was playing what against whom? He hadn't prepared well for Ricky this morning. If King had a game plan, then Rolly needed one too. He looked at his watch. It was 4:30. He had an hour before he needed to leave.

He stripped off his clothes, took a quick shower, put on decent clothes, something acceptable for dinner at the Hyatt with a rich businessman. He took out a notepad and pencil and placed them on the living room table. He picked up a guitar, the sunburst Telecaster. He played for a while, pausing to write down a few notes as he went, things he might want to ask Mr. King Gibson. He started singing a song he'd written soon after he'd begun playing again, after he'd bumped his practice time up to an hour a day.

> *I'm drifting higher and higher above the clouds*
> *I may never come down.*
> *Maybe it's too late*
> *Maybe it's too late*
> *Maybe it's too late to save myself.*

CHAPTER 24

▼

THE HYATT

"What kind of jackass calls himself King?" Rolly said to himself as he drove north on I-5 again. He passed Mission Bay on his left, the manmade dredge-work of water and sandy islands created for Conrad Hilton and his hotel back in the fifties. It was best known now for its annual over-the-line tournament, a softball mutation played by sunburned fat men dedicated to beer, sun worship, and the deification of large-breasted women.

The sky was clear as the sun drifted down towards the horizon, glinting off the glassy smooth water. A man on a jet ski headed in from his last run of the day. Rolly barely noticed, caught up in his thoughts.

He was in over his head. That was for damn sure. Anytime there was a dead genius showing up somewhere other than where he had died, a Chief Visionary Officer taking you out for surfboard lessons, and some mysterious rich guy inviting you to dinner in his hotel suite, something was up. Something bigger than Rolly wanted to handle. It was dangerous.

He popped off the freeway at La Jolla Village Drive, negotiated through the rush hour minivans and Ford Expeditions, and pulled up to the valet parking stand at the Hyatt Aventine. The valet gave his Volvo an impolite look while marking a ticket that he handed to Rolly. Eight bucks. Rolly reminded himself he needed to get a receipt before he left, start an expense account.

The Hyatt was ten stories high, wide and flat, salmon colored, with an arched topping of sea-foam green concrete. He walked into the lobby, across the marble floor, stopped at the reception desk.

"I'm here to see a guest. His name is Gibson, King Gibson."

The young woman at the desk picked up the phone and punched in some numbers. She looked smart. She looked sharp. She was probably a student across the street, at the university, studying molecular biochemistry or something. That's what they studied at UCSD. As far as he knew, Rolly had never slept with a woman who knew anything about molecular biochemistry. As he watched her on the phone, he wondered if women biochemists were any different in bed than women he'd slept with. It was unlikely he'd ever find out. The young woman hung up the phone, smiled at him.

"Mr. King will see you sir. Room 1001. The elevator is around the desk to the right."

"Thank you," Rolly said and headed to the elevator, banning lascivious thoughts of female biochemists, priming himself for his encounter with King.

The elevator doors opened on the tenth floor. There was a small sign etched on the wall in light silver arrows. Room 1000 to the left, 1001 to the right. Only two rooms on the floor. He took a right. The door to the room was open. He knocked anyway.

"Come in, Mr. Waters," a voice responded.

Rolly pushed open the door, stepped into the room. Across a fifty-foot expanse of deep turquoise carpeting, King Gibson sat in a wicker-backed easy chair, facing away from the door, looking out a large picture window towards the setting sun. The late-afternoon sun angled into the room, beginning its dimming.

"Mr. Gibson?" Rolly said.

"Come on in. Have a seat. I'm reviewing the menu."

Rolly took a seat across the table, glanced at Gibson, who hid his face in a large leather-bound menu.

"Would you like something? I'm thinking of the Tournedos of Beef, myself. My wife says it will kill me, all that fat and cholesterol," Gibson said, tapping his shirt over his heart.

Rolly watched the immaculate fingernails, wondering how much it cost to keep them that way. Gibson wore a banker's blue dress shirt, boxer shorts, and thin black socks pulled up to his calves. He had scrawny white legs, old-man legs. His eyes were dark gray, revealing nothing but limitless shallows. His bald head was as white as his legs.

"No, thanks, I've got another date," Rolly lied. It was hard for him to refuse a free meal. He was a musician, after all. But he'd already decided he wouldn't have dinner with King. Eating would divert his focus, distract him.

"Very well. Anything to drink? Beer, wine, bourbon? You look like a bourbon man."

"Just a club soda, thanks. I don't drink," Rolly said, trying to remember what tournedos of beef were, if there was any raw meat or liver involved.

"Good for you," Gibson said as he picked up the phone, "although, I would have pegged you as a bourbon man." Rolly tried to imagine what a bourbon man looked like, wondering if he really looked like one.

Gibson ordered his meal, his voice on the phone a well-practiced mixture of politeness and power, a man who expected his orders to be followed precisely. He didn't overstate things.

Gibson hung up the phone, looked back out the window. Rolly had decided he wasn't going to talk until he heard what Gibson had to say. He could wait. He could stay quiet for as long as anyone. He'd stayed quiet for almost a whole year once. A few high clouds floated by, hinting shades of pink at their edges. Gibson spoke.

"I assume, Mr. Waters, that you have heard of the recent death in the Eyebitz.com family?"

"You mean Mr. Vox?"

"Yes."

"Yes, I'm sorry. He sounded like a smart guy."

"He was indeed, and we shall miss him, professionally, at least."

Rolly waited. King spoke again.

"In truth, he was not an easy man to like, more of a boy really. He was a technical genius, but a social invalid, incapable of working with others without insulting them."

"I understand he had some odd habits."

"Hmm, well, yes. Let's just say he needed someone to keep an eye on him, keep him focused."

Rolly remembered standing outside the office at Capitol Records five years ago, overhearing the A&R rep talking to Matt. Rolly was a big talent, the rep said to Matt, but he needed someone to keep him focused. The rep told Matt he had to take responsibility, keep Rolly in line. Capitol was ready to hand them a check, give them a record deal.

King continued talking, dropping his tone a full fifth of an interval. "Mr. Vox's death makes it more imperative than ever that we recover the item that was lost."

"The Magic Key," Rolly said.

"Yes, the Key," said King. "Have you had any success?"

Rolly was sick of answering questions. It was his turn to ask them. He didn't care how much money King Gibson had.

"Whose idea was it to have Curtis Vox stay at the mansion in The Farms?"

"It was mine."

"Why?"

"As I've explained, Curtis could be unfocused, difficult. I've worked with quite a collection of people in my time, Mr. Waters. I've seen some unusual things. It seemed like a plan that might work well for all of us. Curtis claimed to be happy with the arrangement."

"Do you know a man named G. Tesch?"

"Why do you ask?"

"He's listed as the owner of the house. I assume you know him."

"Yes, I do."

"What can you tell me about him?"

"I fail to see what this has to do with your investigation."

"Probably nothing. I just like to get all the information I can. Sometimes you find a connection later."

"I see."

"Can you tell me anything about Mr. Tesch?"

"Such as?"

"Well, how do you know him? What does he do?"

"Mr. Tesch is a business associate of mine. We have a financial relationship."

"What kind of financial relationship?"

"He manages some of my banking and investment accounts."

"I see. Why doesn't he live in his own house?"

"Mr. Tesch owns several houses, all over the world. He cannot live in all of them at one time."

"Do you know a man named Anthony Kaydell?"

Gibson paused a beat.

"No, I do not."

"He owned the house before Mr. Tesch."

"When was this?"

"About fifteen years ago. Mr. Kaydell was in the computer business."

"I appreciate your attention to detail, Mr. Waters, but I fail to see how any of this relates to the loss of the Magic Key."

"Like I said, it probably doesn't. I just like to cast a wide net. You never know what you might catch with it."

"I understand."

Gibson wasn't shaken, but he might have stirred just a little. Rolly decided to change the subject.

"You said on the phone you had some information you thought I should have?"

"Yes. It's about Curtis."

"What is it?"

"I feel he was susceptible to certain influences."

"Influences?"

"He was an insecure young man. I think certain people may have influenced him."

"Are you saying Curtis didn't lose the key? That he might have given it to someone?"

"Possibly."

"Why would he do that? Wasn't Eyebitz.com going to make him wealthy?"

"There are other things that can influence a young man besides money."

"Women, you mean, sex?"

"I believe Curtis was having an affair with Miss Amati, my secretary."

"Alesis?"

Gibson nodded his head. Rolly processed the new information, wondered if Gibson was the jealous ex-boyfriend type. It seemed unlikely. Alesis had made a joke about marrying a rich geek. Maybe it wasn't a joke.

"It's partly my fault," Gibson continued. "I asked her to check up on Curtis, stop by his house at the end of each day to have him sign papers and things."

"And you think Alesis is connected to the missing key?"

"Probably not, but as you said, it's sometimes useful to cast a wide net. I thought you should know."

"I'll look into it."

"Thank you. I hope I'm wrong. I have always thought very highly of Miss Amati. I've always trusted her."

"How long have you known her?

"A long time, many years."

"Well, It's probably nothing."

"Yes, I'm sure."

There was a knock at the door. Room service had arrived. Gibson turned and waved the waiter in. The man placed a tray on the table between them, lifted the plate cover, revealing glistening medallions of beef. Rolly felt hungry. He took a sip from his soda.

"Are you sure you won't join me?" Gibson asked. Rolly shook his head. Gibson signed the check, tipped the man with a twenty.

"I need to get going," Rolly said.

"You have an appointment?"

"I'm going to take a look around Black's Beach before it gets dark."

"Black's Beach?"

"I just thought I should check out the area where Curtis' body was found."

King Gibson glanced at the fingernails on his right hand, looked back up at Rolly. "Casting a wide net, I suppose?"

"Yes."

Rolly cursed himself for bringing up his trip to Black's Beach. King would want to hear all about it, expect a report. So would Ricky.

"Well, goodnight, Mr. Waters. I do hope you'll keep this conversation between us."

"Of course," Rolly said. He stood up and walked towards the door, glanced back as he opened it. The clouds outside the window were turning to orange. The room was getting dark. He watched as Gibson tucked a large cloth napkin into his collar so it covered his chest. Then Gibson turned to his dinner, stabbing the meat with his fork, slicing off a gentleman's portion and placing it into his mouth. Rolly left the room to the low quiet sound of King Gibson's masticating jaws.

CHAPTER 25

▼

BLACK'S BEACH

Rolly drove into The Farms, past the large granite sentinels, and parked at the curb twenty feet from the private access road that led down to Black's Beach. The road provided the easiest way to get down, but it was gated, off limits to the public. Residents of The Farms all had keys to the gate, so they could drive down, but Rolly would have to walk. Still, it was easier than tramping along the sand all the way up from the Shores.

Technically, it was private property, but this time of day no one would notice or care. He walked past the driveway to Leslie's house and turned onto the road. The gate was padlocked, as he expected. It was only a couple of feet high, so he climbed over it, walked down the steep incline towards the parking lot at the end of the road where it opened onto the ocean.

When he got down, the lot was deserted. In the distance a romantic couple held hands, walking towards Torrey Pines Beach at the other end of the cliffs. A hang glider drifted in the air near the tops of the cliffs, off the glider port next to the Salk Institute. Out on the water sat one lonely surfer, a big guy, looking out at the waves. Rolly couldn't see too well with the sun directly in his eyes, but the guy looked like he was naked. Surfing while naked. That's what Black's was all about. Naked surfing, just being naked. Naked men picking up other naked men. The sun dipped behind a layer of fog that was creeping in a few miles offshore.

Rolly stepped onto the sand, walked up the beach towards the area below the edge of the cliffs where the mansion, the BFH, stood. From the beach, the angle was too sharp and the cliff face too steep to see the house, but he had an approximate notion of where it was located.

A flutter of yellow at the base of the cliffs caught his eye. He headed for it, discovered a taped-off area where the police had been. The yellow tape had ripped and one long piece dangled in the salt breeze. The cops had probably seen and taken everything they could have by now. The scene had been compromised. But it was still worth a look. There might be something the police hadn't noticed. They were working on assumptions Rolly couldn't pretend to have anymore.

He glanced around the sand, crisscrossed it a few times in a pattern he thought he remembered from the chapter in his training manuals about assessing the scene. Nothing. He looked back out to the ocean, the big naked surfer out riding the waves. He seemed to have caught a pretty good one. The waves were larger here, better formed, not like the ones at the Shores Beach board meeting the previous morning.

He looked back at the cliffs where they dropped down to the beach. The area next to the sand fanned out a little. You could climb up on the fanned section before it got steep. He wondered if Curtis' body had bounced at all, hitting the little hillock first, then sliding down to the sand. It was worth a look, if he could get up there.

He lifted one foot, stuck it into a small, flat indentation about three feet off the ground. He reached out, grabbed at a slim crevice, tried to pull himself up. His foot slipped out and he fell on his butt. He got back up, wiped the sand off his pants, noticed a shorter level of hardened sand to his right where he might be able to get a foot up more easily. He walked over, found a foothold, grabbed the rock, and pulled himself up, one foot, then two, until he was standing about ten feet above the beach. He looked around, searching for anything unusual. If Curtis had landed here, anything he was carrying would have come down along with him.

There were several spires of sandstone he couldn't climb over, but he spotted a skinny path he might squeeze around to get behind them. He inched his way along the path, hoping the earth didn't crumble under his feet. He cursed his burrito diet, grabbed one of the spires in a full embrace so he could slide around it.

There was about six feet of space between the spires and the steep face of the cliff. He looked over the area, forcing himself to be methodical, but the dimming light eroded his hopes for any thorough inspection. He saw cracks in the packed earth on the backside of the spires, deep cracks where the soil had eroded away. Looking into the gaps he spotted something white, plastic. He reached out his hand, tried to grab it, but couldn't quite reach. He leaned over farther, straining to get closer, managed to touch it with one finger. The item was flat, about as big as a playing card. He got a second finger on it, pinched it between both fingers, and pulled it out.

It was an Eyebitz.com entry key card, like the one he had been issued by the security guard on his visit to the office. It had the number 0001 printed on it and a picture of Curtis Vox, employee number one, now employee number none. Rolly slid the card into his front pocket, looked into the cracks for anything else he could find, saw nothing of interest. He skirted his way back around the spires and jumped onto the beach. The sun had ducked into the fog bank offshore and the light was going quickly. The naked surfer had apparently come into shore. There was no one out on the waves. Rolly started down the beach back towards the access road. It would be dark by the time he got back up to his car.

A shadow of motion to his left caught his eye, a sudden prickle of skin on his back, a rush of shadow and air. Someone knocked him to the ground. A large, heavy weight held him down. A hand grabbed the back of his head and pushed his face into the sand. He gagged, felt the sand mash into his mouth and nostrils, making it painful to breathe. Fear and adrenaline shot through his body as if he were touching an ungrounded microphone. He tried to resist, pull away from the pressure grinding him down. He couldn't move.

A moment passed. Then another. Whoever had tackled him wasn't saying a thing. Whoever had tackled him was an irresistible force. And Rolly was clearly a movable object. What was the guy waiting for? Was Rolly going to be robbed, beaten? Was he going to be raped by some big naked homosexual surfer?

There was still no sound or movement from the attacker, just a steady, weighted pressure bearing down on Rolly's back and head. The guy could be up there meditating for all Rolly could tell. Maybe this was some kind of new age gang initiation.

So Rolly decided to go with it, relaxed his body, breathed into his diaphragm, gave up struggling. He could wait this out, too. Apparently it was the right thing to do.

"That's good," said a low voice above his right ear. "Let your body relax. Release the tension. When you tense up you make an injury more likely to occur."

The voice above him was high-pitched and raspy, but at the same time soothing and deep, as if Barry White were singing a lullaby to him, backed by Metallica. Sand filled his nostrils. Perhaps he was being suffocated with some secret

Zen technique, the blood slowly cut off from his head by a special Samurai grip. He tried to relax even more.

"Oh, that's very good," said Barry Metallica, or whoever he was. "Now, I have a message I have been requested to deliver to you. Please listen carefully. Are you listening?"

Rolly tried to open his mouth, but could only blow a little sand out in front of his face.

"The message is this. Do not do any more than you have been requested to do. Return that which you do not own to those who do. Do not concern yourself with people and events you know nothing about."

It seemed to be getting even darker than before. Rolly felt groggy, a nauseous swirling.

"Do you understand this message? Can I confirm to my patron that the message has been delivered to the party for whom it was intended?"

Rolly tried to move his head as if to nod yes, felt the back of his neck go numb. A black sticky sheet wrapped around his eyeballs. The sound of the waves grew dim, the fog came in upon him and the sun slipped down below the horizon. And then he felt only darkness, like sleep.

CHAPTER 26

▼

THE EX

The blackness abated. Rolly opened his eyes. It was dark, quiet. There was a scent in the air—flowers. There was a voice in the distance, a woman's voice, humming. It was earthy, angelic, like Mavis Staples on gospel, but lighter and whiter. Something about it was familiar.

He was in a bed. There was a white timbered ceiling above him. His head felt fuzzy, as if he were waking up from a hangover. But he didn't drink anymore. So he couldn't get hangovers. That was impossible.

A beam of light sliced through a doorway into the room, providing just enough illumination for him to review his surroundings. It was a bedroom, definitely, a nice big one, bigger than his bedroom at home. Bigger than his whole house. Something about it seemed familiar, but he couldn't quite put a finger on it.

There was a bathroom off to his right. He pulled himself up to a sitting position on the side of the bed. His head hurt. His back and his left knee were sore, too. He stood up, shaking a little, made it to an upright position, shuffled to the bathroom, switched on the light and looked in the mirror. His forehead had a big red strip down the middle, as if someone had run a belt sander over his face.

Sand. He remembered now, the trip to Black's Beach, the search at the bottom of the cliffs. Someone had attacked him. Someone had jumped him from behind as he walked back along the beach.

He turned and headed back to the bedroom. His head started clearing. But where was he? The light beckoned through the crack in the opposite doorway. He pulled open the door, stepped through.

A large glass coffee table stood on top of a buffed and shiny wood floor. To the left was a large picture window, a tiled patio outside. There were two deep brown leather chairs and a loveseat to match. A large book, *Cuisine de la Mer*, sat on the coffee table, angled a perfect forty-five degrees to the table's beveled corners. It was Leslie's house. Leslie and Joe's house. Somehow he'd made his way here.

If he remembered right, the kitchen and dining room were next. He could hear Leslie's voice. It was she who was singing. He knew what that meant. Most people sing to themselves when they're happy, but not Leslie. She sang when she was agitated, trying to calm herself down.

He started down the hall, lying back in the shadows and watching for a moment as he approached the kitchen. Leslie stood on the cook's side of the kitchen island, punching down dough with her hands, slapping it out on the blonde butcher-block counter. She had her long black hair pulled up and clipped on top of her head. She hummed something familiar, an Eagles song—"Lying Eyes." She used to hum that song all the time back when they were living together, at least whenever she was mad at him. It was her little form of revenge, a not-so-subtle comment on his excuses. Rolly hated The Eagles.

He took a step forward. Leslie glanced up, saw him in the doorway, paused her kneading.

"Rolly! Are you all right?" She had that little flutter in her voice, the one she always had when she worked herself into this state, the one she got just before she started crying.

Rolly smiled weakly, wanting to let her know he was okay, that everything that had ever been wrong with him was okay now, wanting her to stop getting angry with him, which she never would.

"Joe and I were so worried about you," Leslie continued. Well, she might as well spoil it now and bring up Joe. He was the one paying for the house they were standing in.

"Where is Joe?"

"He had an emergency call, had to run up to the hospital."

Rolly sat down at the dining table. "I feel a little groggy still. How did I end up here?"

"We found you on the beach. Joe and I were having our nightly sunset stroll and we found you just lying there."

"Well, I guess that was lucky for me. Was there anyone else around?" he asked.

"No. There were a couple surfers when we first went out. But I didn't see anyone else."

Leslie rolled the dough into a ball, wiped her hands on her apron. She walked around the serving island and pulled up a chair next to Rolly, lowered her beautiful butt into it, looked straight into his eyes. She had that unyielding, earnest look on her face, the one he used to see at least twice a day—when he left the house and when he came home. She still looked excruciatingly beautiful. Soon she would just be excruciating.

"Rolly," she said in a lowered tone, "you haven't been drinking, have you?"

"No."

Her virtuous, vigilant tone drove him crazy. It was the same tone of voice he'd listened to every time he'd come home to her later than she expected, every time he'd shown up hung over and sick, tired of himself and promising he was going to change his behavior. She'd act tough and inflexible, then she'd start crying, as if she were playing both parts in a good cop/bad cop routine. It was an old movie they couldn't stop running.

"I want the truth," Leslie said. The bad cop was talking.

"I haven't been drinking. I haven't been taking anything." Rolly looked her straight back in the eye, something he could never do when he lied to her.

"Joe wanted to call the police, but I wouldn't let him. I made him bring you up here. I just wanted to know for sure." That crying sound came back in her voice, the good cop taking over again.

It was just as well the police weren't involved. He wouldn't have been able to tell them much, anyway. He couldn't have provided a description of his attacker. And the police might have started wondering what a private detective was doing nosing around near the accident scene. Cops put a lot of stock in coincidence.

Rolly rubbed his hand along his knee, realized his pants weren't the khakis he'd put on before leaving his house.

"Where are my pants?"

"I hung them up in the washroom. Your pants were all wet from the tide coming in," Leslie said. "You were halfway in the water when we found you."

"Did you find anything?"

"You mean, did I go through your pockets? Yes, I did."

"What did you find?"

"Your wallet, your keys. Some sort of plastic ID card. That's all." No drugs, that's what she meant. That's what she'd been looking for. Evidence.

"I need to see them."

"Rolly, what's going on?"

"I just need to see them."

Leslie sighed, got up and walked to the washroom, returned with the khakis and handed them to Rolly. He searched through the pockets, found the security card and pulled it out.

"What's that?" said Leslie.

"An employee security card. If you work for this company, it lets you into their building. I found it on the beach."

"You were just lying there, out cold on the beach." The crying tone became stronger.

"Leslie, listen. Did you hear about the guy who fell off the cliffs a couple of days ago?"

"Joe told me something. I don't like to hear about things like that."

"Well, this card is … was, his."

"Shouldn't you give it to the police?"

"Not right now. I need to think about this."

"You're in some kind of trouble, I know it. I know how you are. You can't lie to me."

She was right. He couldn't lie to her outright. She'd spot it in a second, watching his eyes. He had to think now about how much he could tell her, find a way to navigate through it.

"Listen, I can tell you what's going on, but you have to promise not to tell anyone else, not even Joe."

This was the way he could do it, by acting like she was his only confidant. With that she'd hang on a secret forever. She was his co-dependant, his enabler, that's what the relationship counselor called it, back when they had tried couples therapy. She took care of him, watched over him, protected him, controlled him. He never really bought into the new age psychobabble the shrink had spouted, but there were probably some pieces of truth floating around in it, like turds in the ocean.

Leslie looked at him for a moment, mulling her options. She couldn't resist.

"I promise. I just want to make sure you're all right. When I realized that was you on the beach …" Her voice trailed off. That was part of the good cop act, too. Whatever she did was always her sacrifice for him. It irked him now, tweaked his gut. But he missed it too. It was a lot better than having no one in his life. Besides, giving up his secrets, unloading his soul in just the right way used to make her horny. They always had great sex afterwards.

As long as he didn't tell any outright lies, he might be able to slip a story by her. If there was anything he'd learned from all those years together, it was that telling part of the truth was a better plan, by far, than telling none of it, and much more likely to pass inspection. He could leave some things out. The audience only complains about the notes you don't play if they already know how the song goes.

So he told her about his week, keeping to the parts that others would be able to confirm, if she decided to ask anyone. He told her about getting hired by Eyebitz.com, about Fender, the Magic Key, the newspaper story on Curtis Vox. He didn't tell her about the body in the pool, or Moogus getting beat up. And for sure he didn't tell her about Alesis. If Leslie heard anything about another woman, the bad cop would come storming back, she'd start right into that pissed-off place again. Even now, with her life settled and secure with her rich doctor husband, she would get jealous if he brought up another woman.

He finished his story. She made no complaint.

"What happened on the beach, Rolly? You were just lying there."

In his attempt to tell the story just so, he'd forgotten to explain the part that was probably the most important to her, the part she was involved in, the part she'd have to explain to her husband when he got home.

"Well, I don't remember much about that. I found this card on the beach. I was walking back to my car when someone jumped me, knocked me down. That's all I remember."

He left out the warning he'd been given, trying to avoid anything that suggested the mugging had been anything other than a random act. If Leslie decided he was in danger she'd go ballistic, want to call in the police, the sheriff, the shore patrol and the full Navy fleet. She'd secretly call his father, work her act on him. His father didn't want to hear about Rolly's problems. He'd given up on Rolly a long time ago. He just wanted to play golf and boink his young wife once a week on Sunday mornings. If Leslie called Rolly's father, then his father would have to call Rolly and talk to him, pretend that he cared. Or he might call Rolly's mother. That would be worse.

"Who knocked you down?" Leslie asked. She wasn't satisfied yet.

"I don't know, like I said."

He had to lie now, at least a little bit. He didn't know who had mugged him, but he had a pretty good idea. It was that harmonica-abusing, surfboard humping, puka-shelled monkey with the oversized hands. Little Walter.

When he quit drinking, he'd promised himself he'd stop lying, too. But now he had a job that pretty much required lying on a daily basis. For everything he'd done to change his life, here he was again, lying to Leslie in the kitchen while she gave him the third degree, avoiding the truth, figuring out what he could get away with. Sure, it was part of his job. But it didn't feel any different inside.

It made him angry, thinking about it. Perhaps if people hadn't lied to him first, he wouldn't have this problem. Leslie wasn't all virtue herself. Matt had confessed to him, when they were both drunk, driving back to San Diego from Capitol Records, ten minutes before the car left the road. Matt confessed to Rolly about the night he'd been with Leslie.

That was past history. He put it out of his mind. Someone at Eyebitz.com had lied to him, maybe more than one person, maybe every single person he'd encountered there. Except Curtis Vox, who never got a chance. As he thought about Curtis, he realized there might be a way Curtis could talk to him, a way for Curtis to tell him the truth.

"Leslie, I need to call someone. Can I use the phone?"

Leslie gave him the look, the stare, the silence, but her heart wasn't in it.

"You're such an asshole," she said, getting up from her chair. She pointed at the phone. "On the wall, there."

She went back to her bread. She didn't love him anymore, probably hadn't thought about him for months. Until he turned up, lying face down on her beach. It had confused her, set her back into old patterns she thought were gone. But Rolly wasn't her responsibility anymore.

He walked to the phone, punched in the number. He glanced at the kitchen clock. It was almost midnight.

The phone at the other end of the line rang twice. A female voice answered. There were bright and happy sounds in the background, just as always. It was the loft party that never ended.

"Hello," Rolly said. "Is Marley there?"

He waited while the woman went to get Marley. He watched Leslie back at her bread, absorbed in the relentless rhythm of kneading and stretching the dough, building her bread like a fortress against all her unhappiness. He'd gotten fat without her around, but she had stayed slim, hungry, still working hard to control everything. She had little lines on her face he didn't remember, around her eyes and her mouth. It was all for the better. You could see there was a real person there now, with at least one lifetime behind her. There was an aging, imperfect soul beneath that impossible, beautiful face.

He thought about what Matt had told him, the day of the accident, on their way home, what Matt had confessed about Leslie. She had left Rolly the day before, taken her pots and pans and fancy kitchen utensils and cleared out for good. Rolly had never asked her about Matt. It seemed cheap and trivial after what had happened, after everything in his life had come crashing down.

"Hello." A voice responded at the end of the phone, pulling Rolly back from his thoughts.

"Marley, it's Rolly. Have you made any progress with that disk?"

"I'm not going to get anything more without that encryption key."

"What if I could get it for you?"

"How are you going to do that? It's on some computer at Eyebitz.com."

"I know."

"You going to bring the computer to me?"

"Not exactly," said Rolly, twitching Curtis Vox's key card in his hand, watching Curtis' face appear and disappear. "But I think I can bring you to the computer."

CHAPTER 27

▼

A BREAK-IN

Rolly and Marley sat in Rolly's Volvo in the parking lot across the street from the offices of Eyebitz.com. They munched on hunks of fresh-baked bread between sips of licorice-scented health soda. Leslie had been unable to let Rolly leave without forcing some form of sustenance on him. Rolly took his care package, drove downtown, picked up Marley. They arrived at the Eyebitz.com office at 1:30 A.M. No one had gone in or out of the parking lot since they'd arrived. Rolly looked at his watch. It was three minutes after two.

"Sure you want to do this?" he asked Marley.

"Adventure of a lifetime," Marley replied.

Rolly twitched the card in his hand. He hoped it still worked, that no one had deleted Curtis from the system yet. If the card did work, it probably had a unique ID that would get logged on the system. The time it was used would be recorded as well. Rolly wondered if anyone looked through the logs, if anyone would notice a dead man had entered the building just after two in the morning. He realized there might be security cameras at entrances, taking their picture. It was too late to worry about that.

"Let's go," he said.

They climbed out of the car and crossed the street, walked onto the asphalt driveway, stopped at the keypad in front of the gate. Fender had punched in some numbers, but Rolly didn't know the code. Neither he nor Marley were in the best shape for gate climbing, but that's what they'd need to do. He put both hands on the metal bars of the gate, preparing to hoist himself up, looked back to ask for a boost up from Marley. A loud, electrical buzz burst from the lock. Rolly jumped back, bumped into Marley, who stumbled and tripped over the curb. He fell onto the ice plant at the edge of the driveway, let out a loud "Ooof."

"Shit, Rolly. What was that?" Marley rose to his knees.

The gate made a clicking noise. It groaned and started to open. Rolly ran to the wooden fence near the hinge of the gate, crouched down in the ice plant.

"Marley, get up here. Someone's coming."

Marley stood up, ran over and crouched behind Rolly. If they were lucky, whoever was leaving the parking lot wouldn't look back towards them.

Headlights illuminated the driveway. A car engine rumbled and a rhythmic bass thump filled the air. An old Cadillac Coup DeVille passed through the gate, leaving the parking lot. Muddy Waters and Johnny Winter were playing "The Blues Had a Baby" on the car's stereo system. Rolly watched the silhouette of the driver as he passed. One gigantic hand tapped on the steering wheel, playing the downbeat.

Rolly and Marley stayed low, tried to look as inconspicuous as they could for two overweight middle-aged men crouched in a patch of ice plant at two in the morning. The taillights receded, then disappeared along with the music. The security gate stopped, paused in full open position.

Rolly remembered Fender's comment about the slow gate, decided they were better off sprinting than climbing. "Let's go," he whispered to Marley and bolted for the entry. Marley followed. They got inside with room to spare as the gate returned in a slow arc to the locked position. Rolly and Marley paused for a moment to catch their breath. They started up the long driveway.

The building sat silent and still, a looming featureless box in the darkness. It was indistinguishable from hundreds of others that filled up the scrubby brown earth of Torrey Pines Mesa and the valley below it, clinging to the sides of the hills along the freeway corridor, each one a tightly packed container of technological wonders, not like the sprawling old factories of the east coast or Midwest. These buildings didn't produce steel beams or automobiles. They contained a bunch of desks with metal boxes sitting beside them, cathode-ray screens on top of each desk. And inside those metal boxes were millions of ordered electrons, ones and zeros, long strings of digital product created daily by young men eating cheese puffs and tapping on plastic keyboards.

Rolly didn't understand how it all worked, but the order of the electrons made them valuable, so they had to be guarded by other electrons, secret codes, encrypted numbers. Each of these buildings was a chugging, smokeless factory churning out a glowing future where every bit of information, every song and movie and book, would be available to anyone, anytime, anywhere in the world.

But it still required human beings to make it work, people who spent days and sometime nights inside these dull buildings, people with problems and personalities and conflicting ways of seeing the world. People came without warrantees or quality assurance. People couldn't be reformatted and rebuilt once they broke.

"So how do we get in?" Marley asked.

"Around the side," Rolly said, waving his hand towards the left side of the building. They crept along the edge of the building to the side door. There were no lights on inside, no cars in the parking lot. A tiny red LED by the door indicated the spot where the security card should be placed. Rolly pulled the card out of his back pocket, held it up next to the light. The light turned green. The lock clicked. Rolly grabbed the door handle and tugged. The door swung open. They were in.

They paused in the entryway, a small, square room with a concrete floor. Another door stood in front of them. It had a security lock also. Rolly held up the card, heard the door pop, pulled on the handle and walked into the building. Marley followed. If Rolly remembered his tour with Alesis correctly, the room with the computer was just beyond the door on the left.

They waited a moment, letting their eyes adjust to the darkness. The skin on Rolly's arms shone like a pale moon in December. He felt his way along the wall with his hands. He carried a penlight in his pocket, but he wanted to avoid using it until they were inside the room. His left hand bumped against a metal strip, a doorframe. He felt around for the lock, but his hand fell through the doorway. There was no lock, no door, only empty space.

"What's going on?" whispered Marley.

"The door. It's open."

"So?"

"This door's supposed to be locked at all times."

"Are you sure it's the right room?"

Rolly reconsidered, reran the tour with Alesis and Fender in his head. He was sure he was in the right place. But the room was completely dark. Silent. He pulled out the penlight, flicked it on.

The room was empty, except for the twisted remains of the security cage around the computer. The spot where the lock had once been was now a crumpled hole. The metal gate was open, hanging on one hinge. Various pieces of the computer were strewn about the room, a cable here, a circuit board there, as if it had been disemboweled.

"Holy crap," said Marley. "What's going on here?"

"That car we saw leaving. He must have done this."

"Who?"

"Someone who works here."

"But why?"

"I don't know. Take a look through this stuff. See if you can figure out if anything's missing."

Rolly followed with his penlight while Marley picked through the various pieces of the computer, looking them over and assembling them in one central area next to the cage.

"Well, I see one thing missing," said Marley. "There's no hard drive. Everything else is here, but there's no hard drive."

"What does that mean?"

"Well, you can't really store any information without one," said Marley. "It must have had one."

"So he stole it?"

"Somebody did."

"Shhh," Rolly said. He heard something out in the hall. He switched off the penlight.

"What is it?" whispered Marley.

"I don't know," said Rolly. "I thought I heard something. Hang tight while I check it out." Rolly felt his way out the door, turned to his left to face down the hall.

There was a faint blue glow at the end of the hall, dark still shadows, but nothing moving. He listened, heard a faint rapping in the distance, like someone tapping on a glass door. He crept down the hallway, moving towards the center of the building. He passed through the open area where Alesis' code monkeys worked. It was quiet now, with only the low electrical hum of sleeping computers in the air.

There was a large opening ahead where the hallway seemed to get lighter and he realized he was approaching the lobby. He paused by the edge of the wall, revved his courage up, took a peek around the corner. Outside the main glass doors was the dark silhouette of someone peering in. The figure held something in its hand, a long dark tubular shape. It raised the shape up next to its head. A blast of light assaulted Rolly in the face. He wheeled away behind the wall and held his breath. A halo of light danced against the wall in front of him, twitching from one side to the other.

A tapping came on the front door, then a voice, "This is the San Diego Police Department. We've received a silent alarm call for this address. If there's someone in the building, make yourself known. Move slowly and hold your hands in the air."

Rolly waited. It sounded like the officer hadn't seen him, or wasn't sure if he'd seen him, anyway. He held his position behind the wall. He wondered how long the officer would wait. Someone with a key had probably been contacted also. It would only be a matter of time before they opened the building.

"This is the San Diego Police Department. Come out from behind the wall. Hold your hands away from your body so I can see them." Rolly still wasn't sure if the officer had seen him or was just playing a hunch. There was something familiar about the voice. Rolly sat down against the wall, forcing himself to breathe slower, waiting, forcing himself to think it through, to be patient and wait.

He heard a soft pad of footsteps to his left, someone breathing.

"Rolly?" It was Marley.

"What?"

"What's going on?"

"It's the police."

"Shit," Marley said.

The officer called out again. There was a reason the voice was familiar.

"This is officer Bonnie Hammond of the San Diego Police Department. Rolly, if that's you sitting back there and you don't come out in the next thirty seconds I am going to kick your ass."

Rolly turned to Marley.

"Here, take my car key." He bumped into Marley as he stood up, grabbed Marley's hand, and passed him the car key. He pulled out the Magic Key and handed it to Marley, as well.

"Take this, too."

"Who's out there?" Marley said.

"It's a cop. I know her. I'm going to go out there and let her in. While I'm doing that I want you to head out the other door, get back in the car and drive home. Call me in the morning. If I don't answer, I want you to call a guy named Max Gemeinhardt. He's a lawyer, lives in Del Mar."

"Rolly, you've got ten seconds," yelled Bonnie from the door.

"I hope you know what you're doing," Marley said.

"If I knew what I was doing, I wouldn't have brought us here in the first place." He gave Marley a little nudge with his hand.

"Go."

Rolly waited as long as he could while Marley stumbled away from him down the darkened hall, then put both hands over his head.

"Bonnie, it's me. It's Rolly. I'm coming out." He stepped out into the lobby and walked towards the door. He couldn't see her, but he kept walking. A blast of light hit him full in the face from the other side of the right column by the door. Bonnie had taken cover just in case. She turned out the light after confirming it was him. He opened the door and let her in. Her revolver was in its holster, but the fastener on the strap had been unsnapped.

"What the hell are you doing here?" Bonnie said.

"Working," said Rolly.

"At this time of the morning? You know, it's a good thing you told me at the bar you were working a case for these guys. When I saw your face in the flashlight, it looked like you, but I wasn't sure until I put the two together."

"Lucky for me. I guess I set off the alarm. This was supposed to get me in." He showed her the security card, or at least the side of it without Curtis' picture.

"I guess you did. Is there anyone else here?"

"Not that I know of." He hoped Marley had made it to the side door. He would be escaping down the driveway as they spoke.

"So what are you doing here at this hour?"

"Investigating."

"Investigating, huh. What are you investigating?"

"I can't tell you that. Client confidentiality, you know."

"Yeah, I know. I know I'm gonna have to take you down to the station, too, unless someone shows up here to vouch for you." Bonnie might give him some slack, but she'd keep a good grip on the rope.

"It's an internal investigation. They don't want me around the office during regular hours. They don't want me to disturb the employees, make them suspicious."

"Mmm-hmm," mused Bonnie as she shined the flashlight around various parts of the lobby. "I think I should take a look around, anyway. Come on."

"Bonnie?"

"Yeah."

"Someone did break into the building tonight."

"What do you mean?"

"It wasn't me," said Rolly, holding up the security card again. "I got in with this. But I've been looking around. There's some computer equipment that's been messed with."

"Messed with?"

Rolly sighed. He'd hoped that she'd just let him go, not be so thorough. But that wasn't Bonnie. She always did things by the book—almost always, anyway. He needed to show her the computer room.

"Here, I'll show you."

They walked down the hall, Bonnie's flashlight leading the way.

"Kind of weird décor," said Bonnie as the light reflected off a couple of the gargoyles on the blood red walls, the white plastic sides of the code monkey cages.

"Yeah, it's kind of an unusual business here, all around," replied Rolly, wondering what kind of business it really was.

They arrived at the door to the computer room. Rolly switched on the light. There was no need to stand in the darkness.

"I wonder if anything's been stolen," said Bonnie.

"The hard drive," said Rolly.

"Well, whoever did it must have been some kind of neat freak, I guess," said Bonnie, kneeling beside the well ordered parts Marley had laid out.

"I put everything in order so I could figure out what was missing," said Rolly.

"So you were messing with a crime scene and getting your dirty fingerprints everywhere."

"Um, yeah," gulped Rolly. Bonnie sighed.

"Rolly, I'm sorry, but I'm going to have to take you in. You may be telling me the truth about this whole thing. I'm willing to believe that you are, but if I don't follow procedure here I could get myself in deep shit."

Rolly sighed. It had been a long day. It had been a long night. It looked like it was going to be a long morning.

CHAPTER 28

▼

THE LOCKUP

Later that morning, Rolly found himself sitting on an uncomfortable metal folding chair in an interview room of the downtown lockup. True to her word, Bonnie had loaded him into the squad car and booked him into San Diego County Jail. He was tired, depressed, feeling a little unloved. He put in a call to Max, but only got the answering machine. There was no telling where Max might be. Max had retired. He didn't keep office hours anymore, didn't even have an office. He might have gone out early, on the hunt for some rare Mexican hummingbird in Rose Canyon, getting out of the house ahead of rush hour. Or he might be traveling, on one of his minor league ballpark tours. If he was, he'd be out of town for a week, maybe more.

The door to the interview room opened. Bonnie entered, followed by two well-groomed men in gray suits. One of them wore a red tie. The other wore blue. They smelled of oranges and after-shave lotion.

"Mr. Waters, this is Mr. Hayes and Mr. Porter," Bonnie said.

"Hello," Rolly said to them.

"Hello, Mr. Waters," said the man with the red tie. "I'm Mr. Hayes. Mr. Porter and I are investigators for the Atlantic Insurance Company. We'd like to ask you some questions, if you don't mind. Your participation is entirely voluntary."

The man with the blue tie, Mr. Porter, placed a stenography tablet on the table. He tapped a blue mechanical pencil against his thumb.

"What kinds of questions?" said Rolly, looking back and forth between the two men.

"We understand you are a private investigator?"

"Sometimes."

"And you are currently employed by a company known as Eyebitz.com."

"Well, I don't usually give out the names of my clients," Rolly said. Of course, he'd given the name out to Leslie and Marley. And to Bonnie, of course. She must have told these guys. And she must have a reason for telling them.

"We also understand that you were in the offices of Eyebitz.com last night, which is where Officer Hammond arrested you."

There was no sense denying that part.

"Yes, I was in the offices last night."

Mr. Porter reached into his pocket and tossed Curtis Vox' security card on the table, encased in a clear plastic baggie.

"It has also come to our attention that you had this entry card in your possession," said Mr. Hayes.

Rolly glanced up at Bonnie, standing behind the two men. He wondered what kind of trouble he was in now. Bonnie gave him the slightest nod of her head. He decided it was best to trust her, give these guys whatever they wanted.

"Yes, I used the card to get into the building."

Mr. Hayes went back on point. "Can I ask you, Mr. Waters, how you came to possess this card?"

"I found it."

"You found it?"

"On the beach."

"On the beach. I assume you are aware the owner of this card is dead?"

"I read the newspaper."

"Where on the beach did you find the card?"

"I found it at Black's Beach, just north of the access road. I believe it was in the same area where Mr. Vox's body was found."

"Was this just an accident that you found the card, or were you there for a reason?"

"I wanted to see where the body was found."

"Would you be willing to tell us the nature of your work for Eyebitz.com, Mr. Waters?"

"I might be. But first you guys are going to have to tell me what this is all about. Is there some kind of insurance angle?"

Mr. Hayes and Mr. Porter looked at each other, then back to Rolly. Bonnie stood as still as a statue by the door, her muscular arms folded across her chest.

"Mr. Waters, have you ever heard of something called a dead peasant policy?"

"Can't say I have."

"It's not a term my employer prefers us to use. It's a slang term for life insurance policies taken out by a company on its employees."

"You mean if an employee croaks, the company makes money?"

"Yes, if an employee croaks, as you put it, the company is reimbursed for the insured amount."

"This is legal?"

"Perfectly legal, Mr. Waters. Eyebitz.com has taken out a similar policy on all of its employees."

"How much are these policies worth?" Rolly said. He glanced back at Bonnie, but she wasn't giving away anything.

"Not a lot, usually. Forty or fifty thousand dollars."

"Usually?"

"Well, Mr. Waters, I guess that brings us to why we're here talking to you. You see, Mr. Vox was insured for ten million dollars."

"Wow. Doesn't sound like a dead peasant to me."

"Precisely. As you can imagine, Mr. Waters, my company would like to investigate this matter as thoroughly as possible before paying out. As with most life insurance policies, there are conditions under which the policy will not be paid."

"Like suicide?"

"Yes. Also, in this case, any loss of life that occurs through company negligence or while on company property. I hope that provides sufficient explanation for why we're here."

"Yeah, that'll pass. But I'm not sure I can help you."

"Just tell us what you know, Mr. Waters. What are you working on for Eyebitz.com? Why were you at the site of Mr. Vox's death?"

They meant Black's Beach, of course. But that wasn't where Curtis had died. Rolly had been at the original site of Mr. Vox's death. It was in a swimming pool in a mansion at the top of the cliffs overlooking the ocean, not down on the beach. But these guys didn't know that, at least he hoped they didn't, since that would put him at the death scene—both of the death scenes.

"Well," he began, "I can tell you this. I was hired by Eyebitz.com to find something, a key."

"What kind of key?"

"A Magic Key. It's for a computer."

"A Magic Key? What makes it magic?"

"Well, it has some important data on it. Some encrypted code that's critical to the company's business. They're concerned that their competitors might obtain a copy. At least that's how it was explained to me."

"I see. And did this key have some connection to Mr. Vox? Was he a suspect in its disappearance?"

"From what I understand, Mr. Vox had the only copy of the key. He reported it missing and that's where I came in."

"When was this?"

"Sunday morning."

"Did you speak to Mr. Vox?"

"No, I didn't."

"Why not?"

Because he was already dead. That was the truth of it, but Rolly wasn't going to share that bit of information with anyone, not even Bonnie. Not yet. There would be a time for that, but it wasn't now.

"I just didn't get the chance," Rolly said. "I was told by the people who hired me that Mr. Vox could be somewhat elusive."

"Interesting, what did you think about that?'

"I didn't think too much about it. It's a good way to keep getting paid."

"Yes, of course. Mr. Waters, do you know why Eyebitz.com hired you to take this case? It seems a little unusual, given your professional background."

"What do you mean?"

"Well, Mr. Waters, you're hardly the kind of detective one would expect a corporation to hire, now are you?"

Rolly wondered what they knew about his professional background. Had they been watching him, casing his house, following him around? Did they have a whole file on him? They probably knew about his past—the accident, the drinking.

"I have a friend who works for the company. He recommended my services."

"And your friend's name?"

"I'd rather not say. Not if you're going to try and contact him."

Mr. Hayes glanced at Mr. Porter, shrugged his shoulders. Mr. Porter reached into his pocket and pulled out a photograph, placed it on the table in front of Rolly.

"One last question, Mr. Waters," said Mr. Hayes, "do you know this man?"

Rolly picked up the photo. It was grainy, a little out of focus, perhaps taken from a distance with a heavy zoom lens. The man looked about forty, with dark hair and a mustache. It was a picture of Anthony Kaydell.

"I don't think so. Who is he?"

"His real name is Anthony Kaydell. But he probably doesn't use that name, anymore. This picture was taken in Mexico fifteen years ago."

"No, I don't know him."

Mr. Porter pulled out a piece of paper, unfolded it in front of Rolly. It was a sketch of an older man's face, someone in his mid-fifties, maybe sixty years old. He was bald. It was King Gibson.

"Have you ever seen this man?" Mr. Hayes asked.

"No, I don't think so," Rolly lied.

"You're sure."

"I don't think I know him. Who is he?"

"Let's just say he's someone who may have returned from the dead. Is there any other information you would like to share with us, Mr. Waters?"

"I'm done if you are." He wanted to tell them his story, just to get it out to someone else. But he didn't. It was dangerous, but he couldn't resist. He wanted to figure this thing out on his own. He could always remember to tell them something later when it was useful to him.

"Yes, I think we're done," Mr. Hayes said. Mr. Porter pulled a business card from his wallet, handed it over to Rolly.

"Please call us if you think of anything else," said Mr. Hayes. Rolly wondered if Mr. Porter ever said anything. They had a pretty funny routine going for a couple of guys in business suits, clowns with one blue tie and one red. Rolly didn't feel much like laughing, though. Hayes and Porter stood, walked out of the room. Bonnie followed them, locking the door as she left.

▼

CHAPTER 29

THE RESCUE

Rolly stared at the table, wondering what to make of what he'd just heard, the pictures Hayes and Porter had shown him. What did Mr. Hayes mean about the man in the picture—returned from the dead? There must be a connection between Kaydell and Gibson. That much was clear. Perhaps Curtis Vox had committed suicide. Maybe someone had dragged him out of the pool and dropped him off a cliff so the company could collect the insurance money.

The door opened. It was Bonnie again. This time it was Fender who followed her in.

"Well, Mr. Waters," she said, "it looks like you're off the hook. Mr. Simmons here has confirmed that you work for his company. They will not be pressing charges against you. You're free to leave."

Fender leaned against the doorway, massaging his eyebrows, eyes darting up and down at the floor. Rolly got up, walked over to him.

"All right, Fender. Let's go."

Bonnie led them out of the room and back to the check-in desk, where Rolly collected his wallet and flashlight. He handed Curtis' security card over to Fender.

"I guess you'll want this."

Fender took the card, slipped it into his back pocket without saying a word.

"Mr. Waters?" It was Bonnie.

"Yes."

"My pool. What was the name of that guy you suggested?"

"Um, your pool?"

"Yes, I was telling you about the pool at my house. The cleaning guy always puts in too much chlorine. You said you knew somebody."

Bonnie was trying to tell him something, but he was too thick to get it. He played along, decided to figure it out later.

"Oh sure, uh, I'll have him call you."

"Thanks. I hate it when they put in too much chlorine. I'm the only one swimming in it, just one person. All that chlorine, it gets in your system."

Fender and Rolly walked along the long vinyl floor of the hall that led out of the jail. Fender didn't say anything. His deep-sunk eyes seemed to have receded further and further into his skull every time Rolly saw him. Rolly followed Fender out to Fender's car, which was parked in the pay lot across the street.

"That was very uncool," Fender said.

"Going to jail?"

"Yes, going to jail," said Fender. "And breaking into the office."

"I didn't break in. I used Curtis' card."

"Ricky screamed at me for a half hour this morning when he heard about you being in the building last night. He said I was an idiot, a stupid fucking moron. He said it was too bad I didn't fall off a cliff instead of Curtis. He was ready to fire me, and you."

"I'm sorry. How come he didn't?"

"I told him you must have had a good reason for being there, that it had to have something to do with the case."

"It did."

"What?"

"I can't tell you, right now. But I had to look at something myself, when there was no one else around."

"Ricky thinks you're working for somebody else, another company. He thinks you found the key and were using it to steal our programs."

"I'm not."

Fender leaned on the roof of his green Ford Fiesta and stared down First Avenue, as if watching his magical future disappear right in front of him, slipping around the corner of the county building, dissolving away like morning haze in the sunlight.

"Rolly," Fender said, "this could be the biggest thing I've ever hooked up. It's the real thing, like winning the lottery. I don't want to miss out on this one. You gotta help me out here."

Rolly felt angry and tired and beat, but he couldn't help feeling sorry for Fender. Mostly, he felt sorry that Fender had ever thought he could get anywhere in this world by hiring Rolly as a detective. Rolly wasn't a real detective, not like Bonnie, or those insurance guys, Hayes and Porter, slick as Fingerease fret spray. Rolly was a half-decent guitar player and an ex-drunk who'd killed his best friend, then spent three years in the library looking up names in telephone books as his punishment. He was just some guy who'd taken the state exam and set up shop in his mother's backyard. He wasn't smart enough to know when he was in over his head. Not with alcohol. Not with women. And certainly not with entrepreneurial assholes like Ricky Rogers, who could twist guys like Fender and Rolly around like a set of old nickel-wound strings.

Fender was stupid enough to think Rolly was smart. That was the sad thing.

"Fender," Rolly said, "I need to ask you something. You can't tell anyone else what I'm about to say, not Ricky, not Alesis, not anyone."

Fender turned his face back towards Rolly. His eyes were limpid, slightly wet. "What is it?"

"You have to promise not to tell anyone."

"I promise."

Rolly had to put his faith in someone sometime. It might as well be Fender.

"I don't think Curtis Vox died from falling off a cliff."

"What do you mean?"

"I'm just saying I think there's some connection between the Magic Key going missing and Curtis' death. I don't think it was an accident."

"Are you sure? Didn't the police say he fell off the cliff?"

"Yes, that's what they're saying. I'm just not sure they know all the facts."

"You didn't tell them about the Magic Key, did you?"

"No," Rolly said. There he went, lying again. "But I need to ask you, would anyone at Eyebitz.com want to kill Curtis?"

"That's crazy, Rolly," Fender replied. His eyes were dry now. He looked past Rolly, ran his finger and thumb across his eyebrows. "Why would anyone at work want to kill him? He was going to make us rich. He was the brains, the guy that made it all work. Like Ricky says, he'll be impossible to replace."

"Yeah, I know. That's what everyone says. Have you heard anything about life insurance policies at Eyebitz?"

"Life insurance?"

"Yeah, on employees."

"No. We don't even have medical coverage yet."

Fender's inside coat pocket started buzzing, vibrating. He reached in, pulled out his cell phone, looked at the number displayed on the LCD. He took a quick breath, answered.

"Hi Ricky."

Rolly could hear a voice screaming on the other end of the phone. Fender glanced nervously at Rolly, turned away from him. The tirade continued.

"Okay, Ricky," said Fender. "I'll look into it." He pushed the button to end the call, turned back to Rolly.

"That was Ricky," he said.

"Your boss is kind of a screamaholic, isn't he?" Rolly said.

"He's just a perfectionist," responded Fender, looking down at the ground. "We're putting together a deal for this big customer and Ricky doesn't like some parts of the proposal. He wants me to rewrite it. It's just the way he works."

"Well, if you can put up with it."

"Like I was saying, Rolly. The stakes are high. I don't want to miss out on this one."

"I don't think I could take it for long. I'd go back to drinking again," Rolly joked.

Regardless of his proclamations to the contrary, Fender was clearly upset by the phone call from Ricky.

"Rolly, I need to get back to work right away. Can you get a ride home?"

"I'll be fine. There's someone downtown I need to see anyway. Thanks for coming down and getting me out."

Fender opened the door to his car, paused before climbing in.

"What am I going to tell Ricky?"

"Tell Ricky I'll have something for him tomorrow. I promise. He can have his money back if I don't."

"By Leslie's butt and all that's holy?"

"By Leslie's butt and all that's holy."

Fender's demeanor returned to its old goofy self. He smiled, climbed into the car, and drove away, waving at Rolly as he turned the corner.

Rolly walked east on C Street, headed towards Marley's loft. When Rolly had departed from the Eyebitz.com building in the back of Bonnie's squad car, he looked for his Volvo on the street. It was still there. Either Marley hadn't made it out of the building or he'd had trouble getting the Volvo started.

Rolly reached Seventh Avenue and turned down towards Broadway. He saw his car, parked halfway into a yellow zone, a ticket already attached to the windshield. It wasn't exactly a welcome sight, but at least Marley had made it back home.

CHAPTER 30

▼

MARLEY'S VIDEO

Rolly rang the doorbell. Marley looked out from the window above and buzzed him in. He waited at the top of the stairs when Rolly arrived.

"Well, it's a pleasure to see you, Maestro Waters, a free man. The last time I saw you, it was the back of your head moving away from me in a patrol car. What happened?"

"Just a little miscommunication," Rolly smiled. He was tired.

"I guess."

"Can I get that disk back?"

"You bet. Come on in."

Rolly stepped in through the door. The place was quiet. Two children, and a woman who was apparently their mother, snoozed under the blankets on the sofa bed by the kitchen. Marley tiptoed by them, motioned Rolly to be quiet as well. They walked back to the end of the loft. Marley drew the curtain.

"Hey, you need to get that car fixed. It took me half an hour to get it started last night. I thought I'd never get home."

"I know. I've been meaning to take it to the shop."

Marley rustled through the manuals, papers, and CDs that covered his desk.

"I know it's here, somewhere," he said.

"Did you find anything else on the disk?"

"Nothing but that video I told you about. The rest of it's still locked up tight. Ah, here it is." Marley held up the disk.

"The video. Can we take a look at it?"

"It's a little early in the morning for that kind of thing for me, but if you want to."

"I just want to check something."

Marley inserted the disk into the slot in the back of the computer. He clicked on a file in the window that appeared on the screen. Another small window appeared, the video, naked body parts moving, close-ups of engaged genitalia. There wasn't much you could identify. It played for about thirty seconds, then stopped. It meant nothing to Rolly.

"Is there any audio?" Rolly asked.

"Yeah, but I'd prefer not to play it right now," Marley said, nodding his head back towards the rest of the loft. "There's lots of moaning and groaning, and some background music. Actually, the music's pretty good."

"Thanks," Rolly said.

"Thanks?"

"Um, yeah, thanks for showing it to me."

Marley closed the video, pulled the disk from the back of the computer, handed it back to Rolly.

"I'm glad to get rid of this thing. If it's encrypted like that, it's not something they want us to see."

"I'm going to give it back to them."

"Good. The only thing you should be doing at two in the morning is playing guitar. You shouldn't be sneaking around inside of some corporate headquarters. Me either."

"Yeah, I guess so. Thanks for everything. Have you got my car keys?"

Marley rummaged through the piles of junk on top of his desk, pulled out the keys to the Volvo. He tossed them to Rolly.

"Get that thing into the shop, now."

"I will."

Rolly left Marley at his computer and tiptoed back down the hall, out the front door and down to the street. The rest of the block was coming to life. The driver of a delivery truck unloaded cases of beer at the JR Market across the street. Rolly grabbed the ticket off the Volvo's windshield, checked the fine. Sixty-five bucks. He crossed the street to the market, picked up a packet of powdered donuts and a pint of 2 percent milk, returned to his car, and climbed in.

It took him five tries to get the car started. The problem was worse. As he let the car idle, he thought about heading over to Randy's to get the thing looked at.

He ate all his donuts, drank half the milk, then decided against it. He needed some sleep. He put the car into gear and headed for home.

When he got home, he went straight to the bedroom, stripped off his clothes and lay down in bed. His body was tired and sore. He pulled the covers up over his head and fell straight asleep, undisturbed by any dreams, pleasant or fearful.

CHAPTER 31

▼

THE GAME

The phone rang. Once, twice, on the fourth ring the phone machine would pick up. Rolly waited, enjoying the warmth of his covers.

"Hey, are you there?" It was Max, his lawyer. "I called the jail, but they said you'd been released. I've got tickets for the game tonight against the Giants. If you're not doing anything, why don't you come out to the game? You can tell me all about your visit with San Diego's finest. Call me back before six."

Max hung up. Rolly looked at the clock on the night table. It was five-thirty. He stared up at the ceiling and considered the offer.

He walked through the last few days in his head. He'd performed with the band at the mansion above Black's Beach. He'd seen a dead man in the swimming pool, a man whose body later showed up on the beach. Someone had stashed a computer disk containing company secrets in his guitar case. Then he'd been hired to find that computer disk. Moogus got mugged. Rolly got laid. He'd gone surfing, shared room service with a rich old man in a hotel suite. He'd been attacked and verbally threatened by the harmonica-playing director of maintenance for Eyebitz.com, the man he suspected of mugging Moogus, the man he'd seen leaving the Eyebitz.com building just before Rolly and Marley discovered the destroyed computer, a crime for which Rolly had spent four hours in jail.

A baseball game might be just the right thing. That and a visit with Max might be just what he needed. A break. He'd never turned down two games in a row. Besides, Max might be able to tell him something useful about Anthony

Kaydell. Max knew the inside story on every white-collar crime that had taken place in San Diego for the last thirty years.

Rolly's mother met Max back in 1968, the year before she and Rolly's father had separated for the first time. Max had been Eugene McCarthy's west coast campaign manager. Rolly's mom volunteered on the phones at the headquarters downtown. They had stayed in touch over the years, bumping into each other at various liberal fundraising events, like Planned Parenthood and the ACLU. Rolly always figured there'd been something between his mother and Max, but he'd never worked up the nerve to ask either of them about it.

After the accident, as Rolly lay unconscious in the hospital, headed to jail on drunk driving and vehicular manslaughter charges if he survived, it wasn't Rolly's father his mother had called. It was Max. Before the case went to trial, Max made a deal with the District Attorney and the judge, came up with a plan to give Rolly a job in his office forty hours a week. Rolly's mother agreed to take on the rest of the burden, putting Rolly up in the granny flat behind her house, keeping him close at hand, under scrutiny. Between them they had his life pretty well covered. That was how Max became Rolly's lawyer. And how they became friends.

Rolly picked up the phone, dialed Max's number.

"Yeah, who is it?" Max answered.

"It's Rolly."

"So can you make it?"

"Yeah, that's why I'm calling."

"It's the Giants, you know."

The Giants, especially Barry Bonds, always beat up on the Padres. Max didn't care who won the games, but Rolly did. Max loved to give him a hard time about it.

"You know, there's still a statistical chance the Pads could make .500 this year," Max joked.

When you spend your life rooting for a team to achieve mediocrity, like Rolly had done, your hopes could be raised by the slightest improvement on abysmal. That's why Rolly had faith in his team. He'd been to abysmal so many times in his past. He'd come back. Every day now that he didn't drink brought him a little closer to a .500 life. He didn't need to win the World Series.

"Okay," Rolly said, "I'll meet you there."

"Gate J," Max replied.

"Gate J, 6:45." Rolly recited the mantra. Max had some very exact habits when it came to attending games.

"I'm bringing peanuts," said Max. "They're unsalted. I can't stand those ones they sell at the ballpark. They're too salty. And they're a rip off."

That was part of the ritual, too. Max had ten million dollars and he still liked to complain about getting ripped off for a bag of peanuts. He'd been bringing his own bag of peanuts to games for the last twenty years.

At 6:15, Rolly left the house, drove his car down to the trolley station at Morena Boulevard in Linda Vista. He hated parking his car at the stadium. It was cheaper to ride on the trolley. Better people-watching, too. He pulled into the parking lot, locked the car, walked over to the ticket machine, and inserted five dollars. He grabbed his ticket, two quarters in change, crossed the tracks to wait for the next trolley. He felt lighter already. The trolley arrived. Ten minutes later he was at the stadium, walking down the ramp to gate J. Max was already there.

"You're early," Rolly said.

Max shrugged his shoulders. "Traffic wasn't too bad. How's your mother?" It was always the first thing Max would ask. Rolly thought again about his mother and Max. She had been an attractive woman, emotionally worn down at the time. Max was a smooth operator, a good listener, a liberal, all of the things Rolly's father was not. Something could have happened between them.

"She's fine. You got the peanuts?"

Max patted the inside pocket of his coat.

"Unsalted."

Rolly smiled. He was grateful for this small ritual. Some things in life were still dependable, no matter how stupid and crazy the rest of the world might get to be. They headed into the stadium, began talking statistics—ERAs and on-base percentages. One thing that had sealed Max and Rolly's early friendship was their general agreement on baseball matters. Best player, Willie Mays. Best pitcher, Sandy Koufax. That was it. There was no argument.

They talked about baseball through the fifth inning. The Padres were down one-zip in a snoozer. Bonds hadn't hit a home run yet, so there were plenty of chances for heartbreak. Rolly ate an Italian sausage on a hard roll with onions and a plate of garlic fries. He wanted a beer in a tall paper cup. He drank a Coke instead, ate an Eskimo Pie. Max started into his usual rant about the minor league quality of today's major league players.

The baseball talk ended. Max went straight to the next thing on his mind.

"So what the hell were you doing in jail? The cop I talked to said something about breaking and entering?"

"It was nothing, just a little mix up with my client. We got it all straightened out."

"You did, huh?"

"Yeah. He came down to the station, explained it all to the cops."

"Sounded like you might be in some real trouble from that phone call I got."

"No, really, it was just a miscommunication."

"You haven't been drinking, have you?"

"Clean as a whistle, Max. I promise."

"You've been on the wagon for a few years, now. Don't screw up. I don't want to have to bring your mother back down to the courthouse. We're old people, Rolly. We're tired."

"I'm clean, Max. I swear," Rolly responded. Once a drunk, you were always a drunk. The rest of your life was an inquisition. And anyone who knew you—your mother, your ex-girlfriend, your lawyer—was ready to act as your inquisitor. He couldn't blame them.

"So who is this client?" asked Max. "And how'd you get that red stripe on your face?"

"I'm working for an Internet company, here in town."

"An Internet company, huh. Crooks."

"Crooks?"

"They're all crooks. You can just tell. This whole Internet thing is out of control. It's like the gold rush. A few people are going to make a lot of money and everybody else is going to get screwed. It's hype, rich bankers and stockbrokers spinning a fancy money suit out of everyone's greedy dreams. It's like the emperor's clothes, a suit made out of air. Nothing but hot air and magic tricks."

"They're giving me options."

"Well, that's so they won't have to pay you real money. Good. Maybe you'll get rich. But I wouldn't count on it."

Rolly sat back for a moment. Max was contrarian by nature, always acting in opposition to the prevailing mood of the time. He got things wrong sometimes, but not as often as most.

The Giants went out one, two, three. Ashby was pitching pretty well. Tony Gwynn led off the bottom of the sixth, slapped a single to right. There was some mild applause as the fans awoke from their stupor.

"Now there's a real ballplayer," Max said. "How do you pick up private investigation work, anyway?"

"Word of mouth, mostly," Rolly replied, "just like playing music." Of course, most of the mouths he worked for weren't interested in telling anyone about how they'd hired a private detective. You didn't work much as a private eye unless you hustled for business, all of the time. It was just like playing in bands. Rolly was naturally averse to hustling and self-promotion. It hadn't always been that way, but he'd always needed at least one drink in his system to start selling himself to someone else. These days he just wanted to work enough to buy himself time to play the guitar.

"Still playing music?" Max asked.

"Sure, a couple times a week, maybe. A few parties. We still play most Sundays at Patrick's."

"Yeah, I gotta stop by sometime, hear you play again." Max had been saying he'd come hear Rolly play for two years now.

They sat in silence awhile, watching the game. Finley flew out to left. Caminiti struck out, stranding Gwynn at first. It was depressing. Rolly decided to toss a few questions to Max.

"Have you ever heard of a guy named King Gibson?"

Max scratched his beard. "No, I don't think so. Why?"

"Nothing. It's just a name. You know a lot of people in town. How about Anthony Kaydell?"

"Sure. Who doesn't remember that crook?"

"I don't."

"Well, why are you asking then?"

"Someone at the jail asked me about him."

"Has this got something to do with your client?"

"Maybe. There's a house in The Farms that Kaydell used to own."

"Oh sure. The one he sold before he split town."

"Yeah. My client seems to have a connection with the current owner."

"Who's that?"

"Someone named G. Tesch. He bought it from Kaydell."

"He must have been the one they tried to sue."

"Who?"

"The investors. This Tesch guy, he was from Barbados or something. The stockholders tried to get the court to revoke the sale of the house, but it was legit. There was nothing they could do."

"Do you remember anything about Tesch?"

"Tesch and Kaydell did the deal privately. No one else was involved. No one knew who Tesch was or what he looked like. The D.A. looked into it, but there wasn't much he could do. Tesch had lawyers. He wasn't a U.S. citizen. A lot of people think there was something fishy there, though."

The Giants put men at the corners. One out. Rolly sat watching the game without seeing it. He had a new set of chord changes to play with, but the melody was still incomplete. Where was the hook? A man named G. Tesch owned the house Curtis Vox died in. Gibson knew Tesch. Kaydell sold the house to Tesch. But no one else knew anything about him. What was the connection?

"The BFH," Max laughed, scratching his beard, staring out towards the scoreboard above right field.

"The what?"

"BFH. The Big Fucking House. That's what they called the house in the D.A.'s office. There was a story going around that Kaydell put up the money to produce a porno movie, that it was filmed at his house in The Farms."

Rolly's stomach jumped up and rumbled like there were two tom-toms inside it, playing a Bo Diddley beat. Max continued.

"They got a copy of the video, passed it around the office. I don't think they ever did much with it. There was no connection to the case. The attorneys started calling it the BFH, the Big Fucking House. I think it's a line from the movie. It was their little joke."

Rolly had a pretty good idea who the star of the movie was.

"Max, I need to go. Can you give me a ride to my car?"

"What's your hurry?"

"I just need to go now."

"Hey, the game ain't that bad. The Pads could still turn a double play." Even as Max spoke, the Giants batter sliced a single to left, bringing in the runner from third. Max laughed.

"Ah well, maybe you're right. I need to get up early tomorrow, anyway. I'm going birding down at Border Field Park." Max rose from his seat, followed Rolly, who was already halfway up the aisle, moving faster than usual.

"Hang on, I'm an old man," Max said.

The walk to the parking lot took forever. Half of the crowd was leaving the ballpark. Rolly worried that he and Max would get stuck in the traffic. He climbed into Max's Mercedes coupe. Max turned on the engine, looked at Rolly.

"Rolly, I'm your lawyer, you know. Anything you say to me is confidential. If there's something you need to tell me, I think you should do it now."

"I'm okay, Max."

"I don't know who you're working for, but you'd better be careful. If this has something to do with Anthony Kaydell, you are in way over your head."

"I'm okay."

"I don't want to have to call your mother if something happens to you."

Rolly didn't say anything. Max put the car into gear and headed out of the parking lot. It looked like they'd beat the rush.

CHAPTER 32

▼

THE VIDEOTAPE

Max dropped Rolly at the trolley station. Rolly got into his Volvo, started it up and headed towards Moogus' place in Ocean Beach. He needed to look at the videotape, "New Wave Nudes," starring Alesis Amati. There was something in the movie, something that just might explain this whole thing, something about the big house that Curtis had lived in, had died in, some connection to Anthony Kaydell, G. Tesch.

He pulled the car onto I-8, headed west, took the exit marked "Beaches." He drove along the long causeway that ran along the outflow from the San Diego River. Fresh water mingled with salt from the ocean, transforming from river to sea. He remembered the odd conversation with Bonnie this morning as he left the jail, her mysterious complaint about the chlorine-happy pool man. Bonnie and Joan didn't have a swimming pool.

Then he realized what Bonnie had been trying to tell him. It was the chlorine. Bonnie knew that someone had called in with a report of a body in the pool at the house in The Farms. Now the autopsy had confirmed it. It was Bonnie who had been on patrol that night, had responded to Rolly's 911 phone call. She knew, for sure now, the call wasn't a hoax. Curtis Vox had been in the pool. He had been there, and someone had moved him. Rolly knew it. Bonnie knew it. And so did one other person, at least. Bonnie was testing Rolly, trying him out, angling to get something back. He hoped to have something for her soon.

He pulled up to Moogus' house, a two-room shack three blocks from the beach. He knocked on the door.

"Moogus, it's Rolly."

Moogus opened the door, dressed in boxer shorts with a big smiley face on them, a green Zildjian t-shirt, scratching his belly. The area around his left eye was multicolored green, with a bit of purple towards the nose. There was a girl with blond hair, a beach rat of indeterminate age, lying on the sofa, watching TV.

"Hey, Rol, what's up?" Moogus said.

"I wanted to pick up that videotape."

"You miss her already, huh? I was planning to bring it over to you tomorrow, but you're just too hot for it, I can see. I got it right here."

Moogus glanced back at the girl.

"Hey, throw me that tape there, would you honey?"

The girl looked up at Moogus, glanced over at Rolly with deeply stoned eyes, then reached over to the table at the end of the sofa, picked up a videotape and tossed it to Moogus, who dropped it. Moogus leaned down, picked up the tape from the floor, handed it over to Rolly.

"Let me know what you think. The soundtrack's not bad considering the band was stoned out of their minds. Sideman sucks less than usual. Of course, you won't be paying much attention to the music."

"Thanks," Rolly said. He grabbed the tape and ran back to his car.

"I hope you'll still respect yourself in the morning!" yelled Moogus as he stood in the doorway, laughing. The pale blue light from the television formed an aura of light around his body, as if the moon was hiding behind him, a Moogus eclipse.

Rolly put the car into gear and headed downtown. A high layer of mist rolled in from the ocean, across Coronado Island. His father's house would be under it now. The fog stretched its fingers in lingering filaments across the bay, touching the tops of the skyscrapers that lit up the downtown skyline. It was beautiful, unknowable. He thought about parking down at the Embarcadero, by the *Star of India*, the old whaling ship. He wanted to watch the clouds touch the tops of the masts, then roll down the ropes and settle in silence around him.

But he didn't have time for that. He had to go watch a dirty movie.

CHAPTER 33

▼

AN INTRUDER

Rolly opened the front door of his house, turned directly to the TV in the corner, intent on playing the video, sure there was some clue hidden there, if only it could be found and deciphered. He slapped the tape into the VCR, grabbed the remote. There was a noise in the bedroom behind him. He stopped, turned around.

The room was a wreck. Someone had opened his guitar cases, dumping the contents all over the floor. Other guitars had been knocked off their stands or pulled down from the wall. His Epiphone and his Stratocaster. His Martin Dreadnought and Les Paul. His sunburst Telecaster leaned against the wall at a dangerous angle. And worse, much worse, his precious ES-335, a big divot dug out of the finish, lay at his feet.

He knew he should leave, make a run for the door. Someone was here, someone dangerous. Instead he stood in the middle of the living room, unable to move, feeling violated, raped, defiled. He'd been beat up and lied to. He'd landed in jail. But this was beyond the limits of what he could stand. Someone had messed with his guitars.

A bulky silhouette filled the bedroom doorway. It was Little Walter, looking even less little than usual and moving towards Rolly more quickly and quietly than Rolly would have thought possible for a man of that size. For some reason all Rolly could focus on was the necklace of puka shells dangling from Walter's thick neck. He took a step back, but it was too late. A loud crack rang in his left ear. He found himself face down on the floor. Something wet and warm drained onto his tongue from the back of his mouth. He hated surfers.

"Sir," Walter began in his odd voice, "I have the highest respect for musicians. I admire all artists, as I play an instrument myself. I did not wish to damage your instruments and I do not wish to hurt you. But my employer has requested that I return to him a certain article that he still believes you have in your possession. I have actively chosen to honor my employer and act upon his needs. So I will ask you directly—where is the Magic Key?"

Rolly pushed himself up to his knees, looked out towards the front door. It was only ten feet away. If he could just get outside, maybe someone would see him. He lived in the heart of a crowded metropolis, in Hillcrest, where the boys were out cruising all night. There was always someone in the neighborhood, passing through on their way to the bars and the restaurants.

A large hand grabbed him by the back of his hair. Another large hand slapped him on the right side of his face, over his ear, then on the left. His head started ringing. The room twisted, went sideways. It felt like he was drunk, except for the pain.

"Where is the key?" Walter put his face down next to Rolly's. "I wish to honor my employer's wishes. I have made a vocal commitment to him to return with the key."

Rolly gurgled, tried to get his bearing, pull himself together, focus inside and think clearly. He tried to scream. What came out of his mouth surprised him.

"Mom!" he screamed. "Mom!" It was as if someone else were screaming, a boy he knew a long time ago.

"It is childish of you to call for your mother," said Little Walter. "You are an adult, with adult responsibilities. You must renounce your childhood. You must leave it behind." He threw Rolly to the ground, put his knee in Rolly's back, grabbed Rolly's arms, and twisted them back in their sockets. It was painful, but at least it pulled Rolly's head up so he could see something more than four square inches of wood flooring. The front door was still open, although with the light out, no one was likely to see them inside.

"I would like to inquire again as to the whereabouts of the key," Walter went on, still pulling on Rolly's arms.

Rolly hung on through more pain than he would have thought possible. To his left he saw the ES-335, face down. The tuning head was about two feet from his face. The top left tuning peg was bent at an angle, the wood split where it had been screwed into the head. To think that this guy liked to call himself a musician, messing up a perfectly good guitar like that.

It was hard to breathe. There wasn't any air he could pull into his lungs. Or maybe it was just that his lungs couldn't move, Little Walter's knee planted as it was in his back.

"Rolly?"

Someone was calling his name, a high sweet voice, like Minnie Ripperton returning from heaven or wherever she was now.

"Rolly, are you all right?" said the voice.

The pain in his arms released a little as Little Walter looked up. He'd heard the voice too. It was real. It wasn't Minnie Ripperton welcoming him into the next life. Walter took his knee from out of Rolly's back, stood directly above him.

"Rolly?"

He knew now it was his mother. She'd heard him scream. She was outside on the gravel driveway, walking towards the front door. She was going to walk straight into Little Walter if Rolly didn't do something. This was his chance. He might not get any more. He reached to his left as slowly and quietly as he could, felt the top of the ES-335, the steel strings under his hand. He closed his hand around it, made peace with himself for what he was about to do, coiled his body and swung the guitar around with all he had left in him.

A scream filled the room as the maple wood body of the guitar crashed into Little Walter's left knee. The guitar made a sickening sound as the wood cracked and shattered. Walter crumbled to the floor like an old eucalyptus in an El Niño windstorm.

"Rolly!" His mother ran towards the house. He could hear the scrunching of gravel.

"Auugh, fuck it, fuck it, you fucking hack, you fucking junkie!" screamed Walter. He was lying on the floor, but turning towards Rolly. Rolly stood up, the neck of the guitar in his hand, the rest of it splintered around him. He looked around for another weapon. The gold-top Les Paul was closest, a good ten pounds of solid mahogany. With the right amp it would let you sustain a note forever. Walter reached out with both hands, his gigantic surf-paddling, harmonica-mangling hands. He grabbed tightly onto Rolly's left ankle. Rolly grabbed the Les Paul, brought the guitar down on Walter's back. There was another sickening crack and a grunt. Walter's grip remained strong. Rolly swung again. The guitar glanced off Walter's shoulder and into his head. He stopped moving. His hands loosened and fell to the floor.

"Rolly, what's happening?" His mother stood at the door. Rolly moved towards her, turned on the light. His mother's face went white when she saw him.

"Rolly, what's going on?"

"Call the police, Mom. Call the police."

His mother's eyes were wide open, terrified. She looked past him at the body on the floor.

"Who is that? What happened?"

Rolly paused for a moment. His heart beat incredibly fast. He could hear the blood throbbing close to his still muffled eardrums. He looked down at the mountainous body stretched out on the floor, shards of his ES-335, the guitar that had saved his life, scattered around it.

"It's just some harmonica player. Call the police. Tell them to bring an ambulance, too."

Rolly knelt down by Little Walter's shoulders, reached for the puka shell necklace, ripped it from his neck, and threw it into the corner of the room, a little revenge for the defilement and destruction the man had brought to the room. Little Walter lay still. Rolly couldn't tell if he was living or dead. He didn't care. The man had been caught breaking and entering. Rolly had the law on his side this time, clear as day. He reached into Walter's left pocket, pulled out a pair of keys attached by a ring to a small plastic block, a car lock remote. Each key had a small piece of masking tape stuck on it, one labeled "car," one labeled "house." You had to wonder about the mental capacity of a man who needed labels to tell two keys apart. Rolly tried the other pockets, found nothing. He had to give Walter credit for that. His hands were his only weapons. No knives or guns or brass knuckles.

Ten minutes later, the police arrived. The paramedics joined in half a verse later. Little Walter lay still on the floor, like a big Kahuna who'd drunk too many Mai Tais. The paramedics grunted and strained as they lifted him onto the gurney. Rolly answered the policemen's questions, denying he'd ever seen Little Walter before, keeping to the simplest, truest story he could. He'd been to the baseball game. When he came home, the guy had been here, had jumped him. These guitars were worth a lot of money, you know. And look what this guy did to them. Rolly gave them a little outrage, a little hysteria to make it look like he was a complete innocent. He said nothing to suggest this event was not unexpected, considering what had happened to him in the last seventy-two hours of his not quite break-even life.

The police finally left, but not without turning down several offers of tea and soy cookies from Rolly's mother, who stood by the door in her nightgown and slippers the whole time. After the police departed, she and Rolly spent thirty minutes cleaning up, talking themselves down until the adrenaline started to fade. He walked her back to the big house, sat for another fifteen minutes in her kitchen, sipping on herbal tea of some sort until he could tell she was ready for sleep. He walked back to his flat, lay down on the sofa, flipped on the TV, inserted the videotape into the deck. He picked up the remote control and pressed the play button.

CHAPTER 34

▼

THE BFH

An hour later Rolly found himself driving north on I-5 again, but this time he cruised along in Little Walter's big Coup DeVille. He was headed to La Jolla, to The Farms, to the Big Fucking House where this whole thing had started. The Magic Key lay in the passenger seat, it's digital secrets still unrevealed. But Rolly had hope. Or something like it. He had Walter's house key in his pocket and a whole new idea about what Curtis Vox might still be able to tell him.

The videotape had been unrevealing at first, if you could call it that, since most of Alesis was revealed throughout. Rolly found it hard to focus, at first. The battle with Walter, the pictures on his TV; they jangled his hormonal balance in ways that were slightly disturbing, as if he were eighteen years old again. Violence, victory, and sexual display. It was a lot to absorb in one evening, riling his blood, raising his measure. He finally gave up, took care of personal business, then rewound the movie to watch it again, calmer, clear-eyed.

Some of the scenes looked familiar. The film had definitely been shot at the house in The Farms. One exterior shot by the pool looked similar to the layout of the yard that Rolly remembered from the party. And the background of a couple of shots was clearly the main hall. There wasn't much background to look at in most of the shots.

He found the scene that had been on the disk, the one that Marley had shown him. Curtis Vox must have put it there for a reason, something besides an infatuation with Alesis, something besides the fact that he was a young, horny geek, without any friends, who lived in a house that was too big for one person and felt lonely at night. Curtis liked to play games, create puzzles, that's what Professor Ibanez had said. Rolly closed his eyes and listened to the movie's music track, playing the notes back in his head, the notes he'd put on tape fifteen years ago during a session he still couldn't remember. He paused and rewound the scene over and over, inspecting each frame. Then he found what he was looking for, a slight glimmer, a few frames of screen time, a little hint in the dangerous game that Curtis Vox had been playing.

He called Bonnie at the station. She didn't answer, so he left a message on her voicemail. He made a joke, invited her to a pool party at the big house in The Farms, suggested she meet him there in an hour or so. He picked up his car keys, checked to make sure the Magic Key was still in his pocket, and walked out to his car.

But his car wouldn't start. The old Volvo wagon had finally died. It wasn't going anywhere without a tow.

Rolly had Walter's keys in his pocket. He got out of the Volvo, looked around, tried to guess where Little Walter most likely had parked. He walked through his mother's backyard, took a right along the fence out to Eighth Street. The street to his left was quiet and dark, three blocks that led to a cul-de-sac. It would be a good place to hide the big Coupe DeVille. He started down towards it.

As he reached the end of the street, he pressed the button on the remote pad. A car horn honked, headlights blinked. It was Walter's car, wedged in between an old Ford Fiesta and a new Volkswagen Beetle. Walter had tried to park parallel, but hadn't quite managed it. The big headlights of the Coupe stared out at Rolly from its cramped parking spot as if looking for a getaway. A car like that needed room.

Rolly opened the door and climbed in. He slid into the frictionless seat, put the key into the ignition, and started the engine. The stereo came on, blasting away like cold vengeance, Paul Butterfield playing "Who do you Love?" Rolly jumped, stabbed at the controls, trying to turn the thing off. He finally hit something that lowered the volume.

He slipped the car into reverse, turned to look out the back window. It would be tight getting out. He tapped on the gas pedal, a little too much, felt a small bump as he touched fenders with the car behind him. He turned back around, cranked the wheel, and put it in drive, clearing the Volkswagen in front by less than an inch.

The drive to La Jolla was easy. He'd been up this way so many times in the last week, he could do it without even thinking. The events of the last several days ran through his mind, unedited, like his father's old slide shows of family vacations. Except Rolly was the man with the camera this time. He didn't appear in the snapshots, only the sights that he'd seen.

He took the exit to La Jolla Village Drive, turned left. There were very few cars on the road. The traffic lights ahead of him all turned to green. As he sped up the hill, he noticed a pair of headlights pinned to his rearview mirror. He drove past UCSD, then turned into the entrance to The Farms. The headlights still followed. He slowed the car down as he turned onto Starlight, crept past the bougainvillea-wrapped walls of the indifferent mansions. He pulled into the driveway of the BFH. The headlights pulled in behind him. Rolly turned off the engine, opened the door. He jumped out, turned to look at the car that had followed him.

It was a green Ford Fiesta, the engine still idling. There was a small dent in the front fender. Sitting inside, staring out from behind the steering wheel, looking surprised and confused, was a face that he knew.

He walked over to the Fiesta, yanked at the handle on the driver's side door, pulled it open.

"Get out, Fender. Get out of there, now."

Fender looked up at Rolly as if he were sick. He turned off the engine, reluctant and guilty, caught in a cognitive dissonance as noisy and dense as a Captain Beefheart LP.

"Rolly, what are you doing here?"

"The question is what are you doing here, Fender?"

"I ... I thought you were Walter."

"Walter's not feeling well. I borrowed his car."

"What happened?"

"Walter's in the hospital. He tried to kill me. He trashed my house, my guitars."

Fender looked out through his windshield, away from Rolly.

"You were there, weren't you?" Rolly continued, suddenly seeing the Fiesta again, parked behind Walter's Coupe DeVille back in Hillcrest.

"He made me do it, Rolly. He threatened me. He told me he just wanted to talk to you. I didn't know what else to do."

"You were there."

"He made me stay. He said I couldn't leave until he got back, that he was going to take care of things, once and for all. I had a headache. I was tired. I put the seat back and shut my eyes. The next thing I knew, Walter's car had bumped into mine and was driving away. I thought you were Walter."

"So you followed me here."

"Yes. He told me I had to stay with him. I didn't know it was you. You have to believe me."

Rolly couldn't afford to believe anyone now, but Fender's story was not without logic or sense.

"Is this what he wanted?" Rolly said, pulling the Magic Key from his pocket, brandishing it in front of Fender's face.

"Rolly, you found it! That's great!" Fender reached out his hand. Rolly stepped back.

"Why did Walter come to my house?"

"He wouldn't tell me. He said he had to talk to you. He told me he'd kill me if I told anyone else."

Rolly looked at Fender, his anger fading. Fender was scared. Fender had lived in fear his whole life, of schoolyard bullies, of women and sex, of bosses who demanded impossible things. Someone like Little Walter would make him crap in his pants.

"I can't give the key back yet. There's something in this house I need to find."

"What do you mean?"

"There's more to this than just the lost key. Curtis had some kind of secret, something he was trying to say."

"Curtis?"

"Yes." Rolly held up Walter's keys. "I think this is a key to the house. I think that if Curtis' computer is still in the house, it has something on it that will explain everything."

"What do you mean, explain everything?"

"I can't tell you, right now. But I'm going into the house. You can come in with me or leave."

Fender looked out at his windshield. He ran the thumb and forefinger of his left hand along his eyebrows, stroking them. His right hand still clung to the steering wheel, shaking a little. He made a decision, pulled his hand off the steering wheel, turned off the headlights. He stepped out of the car. He acted like a man who'd found new resolve.

"I got you into this, Rolly. I should go with you."

They walked to the front door. Rolly inserted the key, turned the lock. The tall, heavy door swung open into the hall. Through the tall windows across the room, you could see the lights from downtown La Jolla, twinkling jewels set in the indigo ocean, peeking out through the fog. The lower edges of coastline had disappeared in the creeping gray layer of mist. It wouldn't be long before the whole coastline was shrouded in fog all the way up to the cliffs.

"So you got any idea where Curtis kept his computer?" Rolly asked Fender.

"In the bedroom. Down at the end, up the stairs," Fender said, leading the way. They crept down the hall, past the door that led onto the deck, and up the stairs to the room overlooking the pool. It was dark in the room, but a tiny green light shone out like a beacon. A computer was there. It was still powered up. Rolly stepped towards it, ready to unlock the secrets of the Magic Key.

▼

THE PROGRAM

The computer's monitor sat on top of a large melamine desk, the computer case on the floor down below it. There was a king-sized bed next to the desk, a set of closet doors along the opposite wall, an open door that led to the bathroom. Rolly walked to the desk, tapped the keyboard. The monitor's screen flickered to life. He got down on his knees, crawled under the desk. He pulled out his pen-light, flipped it on, and directed the light at the back panel of the computer case. There were several odd looking connectors, but one of them looked about the right shape and size. He slipped the Magic Key out of his pocket and pushed the end of it up against the connector, jiggled it a little until it slid into the slot. He pulled himself out from under the desk, rose to his knees, and looked at the screen. The Eyebitz.com logo appeared on the desktop. He grabbed the mouse, double-clicked on the icon to open the disk, then double-clicked on the icon labeled "Start." Up popped the message he'd seen on Marley's computer—"Computer unknown. Encryption key not available." He clicked the "Close" button. He had been sure the Magic Key would work on Curtis' computer. There was still something missing.

"Doesn't look like it's working," Fender said as he sat down on the edge of the bed.

"No," Rolly said. He looked through the listing of files on the disk, a long list of numbers, trying to remember which one was the video file. He found one numbered 696969, double-clicked on it. Up came the video. Curtis might have had an IQ equal to Einstein, but his EQ was predictably Beavis and Butthead. With the video playing, Rolly tried double-clicking the start icon again. A blank window popped up. The computer churned for a couple of seconds. Then a new message was displayed.

Encryption accepted. Waiting for hard drive insertion.

"What's that mean?" Fender asked.

"I don't know. It's progress, at least."

Rolly was at a complete loss as to what he was supposed to do next. What needed to be inserted? Another disk? No one had said anything about a hard drive. He stared at the screen for another minute, puzzling it out in his head.

"Rolly?"

"Yeah."

"Is it okay if I go to the bathroom?"

Rolly looked over at Fender. "Go ahead."

Fender got up off the bed and shuffled to the bathroom door, closed it behind him. Rolly's knees were beginning to ache, so he stood up. He walked to the sliding glass door that led to the balcony overlooking the pool. The moon shone on the dark rectangular surface of the water below. The answer was close. He had all the chords to the song now, had arranged them in order and played out the notes, but the arrangement was all in his head. He had to find a way to get it on paper, on tape, so that others could hear it, respond. He rubbed his eyes, looked at the reflection of himself in the glass. An idea popped into his head.

He walked back to the computer, replayed the video, paused it right at the critical frame. There was the face, the key to it all, reflected in green light in a glass door in the background of the scene. It was an amateur, cheap-budget mistake that hadn't been edited out. It wasn't much, too small to identify on this tiny screen, but clear as day in the original video. It was the uneasy face of Anthony Kaydell, reflected off a glass door. He stood off to the side of the action, watching another man give it to his girlfriend, or whatever Alesis had been. Waiting for hard drive insertion. God, that was it. Rolly looked at the scene, the action stopped just at a critical moment, with Kaydell's face, yes, King Gibson's face, floating above the action like some sleazy Wizard of Oz staring down at his dirty bitch Dorothy. Rolly grabbed the mouse, moved it across the screen and, holding his breath, clicked on the critical anatomical spot.

The message on the screen disappeared, the video too. The monitor screen faded to black. The face of King Gibson appeared on the left side, a picture of

Anthony Kaydell on the right. The two faces crossed the screen towards the center, merging together like something from a cheap science fiction movie. The two faces became one and the same. Then the picture of Gibson/Kaydell got smaller and moved to the upper left corner of the screen. On the right side appeared several scrolling paragraphs of illuminated text.

> I, Curtis Vox, Chief Technology Officer for Eyebitz.com, have recently discovered that the company I work for has become nothing more than a sham, an illegal money laundering operation for a man known as Anthony Kaydell. Mr. Kaydell has been missing since 1985, shortly after he stole millions of dollars from investors who had given their money to him. Mr. Kaydell now works as Executive Vice President for Eyebitz.com and goes by the name of King Gibson. What follows is a list of banking transactions I have found, whereby money has been transferred from Mr. Gibson's accounts into the Eyebitz.com business account.

There followed a listing of dates, account numbers, and dollar amounts, a dozen or more. The narrative continued.

> Mr. Gibson has been granted hundreds of thousands of stock shares by our fearless leader, Ricky Rogers, in return for Mr. Gibson's investment and "consulting services" with the company. I believe it is King's intention to sell his shares as soon as the company goes public. He will get millions in a legitimate payout in return for his investment with Ricky. The dirty money from his offshore bank account will disappear and be replaced by legal tender deposited in a legitimate U.S. bank.
>
> I was hired to work for Eyebitz.com by Ricky Rogers, who attended a Linux User's Group meeting where I demoed my video player. As far as I know, he is unaware of the true source of the money supporting this company. I have come to the conclusion that Ricky is nothing but an egotistical weenie who lives under the hallucination that he is some kind of great new age business guru, when, in reality, he is nothing more than a professional shithead and a shinola salesman.
>
> There is something that only Ricky, King Gibson, and I know about. My algorithm is fake. It doesn't work. It's nothing but a programming parlor trick, something I put together from bits and pieces of open source code. I've built my own shell around it to hide the real thing. That's the real reason we limit access to the compression machine, so that no one gets enough time to figure out how it really works. I knew it right from the start, of course, but told Ricky and King only a few weeks ago. I thought I could program some-

thing that really works, but I can't, not in the timeframe they've set for our IPO.

I have tried to convince Ricky we could spend more time and, in another six months, have a product that really works. But he will not listen to me. He keeps saying we can't bail out on the big wave now, whatever that means.

I think some of the other programmers have begun to suspect. But no one is talking. They all want to believe. They all want to get rich. Just like I thought I did.

I realize now I have created a monster. But I do not have to continue to keep it alive. As of today, I'm going to stop working. I'm going to sit here in this house and take the paycheck they give me. Gibson knows if they fire me, I'll make this information public. All it takes is one click of a mouse.

<u>P.S.</u> Gibson sent that slut secretary over to "talk" to me yesterday. I resisted this time. It's an old movie I've seen too many times. Also, I bought a gun. Just in case that stupid ox Walter comes nosing around.

That was the end of the message, except for a button marked "Do It." Rolly rolled the cursor over the button, watched it light up, wondered what would happen if he clicked it. Where would the information be sent? The newspaper? The police? Mr. Hayes and Mr. Porter from Atlantic Insurance? Curtis Vox had been one clever little geek, equal to almost anything Ricky or King Gibson could ever have thrown at him. Almost anything, except maybe murder. Rolly's finger lingered over the mouse. Maybe he should just click the button, send the information wherever it was supposed to go, put an end to this thing once and for all.

A noise turned his head from the screen, a clunk from the direction of the bathroom. It was Fender.

There was a dark shape in the Fender's right hand. It was a gun, raised and pointed at Rolly. Of all the stupid, unbelievable things Rolly had witnessed in the last week, this was by far the most stupid and unbelievable of them all.

CHAPTER 36

▼

THE STORY

Rolly didn't move, keeping his index finger frozen above the mouse. He kept his voice low, conversational, as if Fender pointing a gun at him was not an unusual event. In a way that he couldn't quite understand, he felt calm. Scared, but calm.

"Fender, what are you doing?" he said.

"Take your hand off the mouse." Fender's voice was high-pitched, barely contained. It was hard to tell which of them was more frightened.

"I know what's going on now, Fender. There's nothing you can do. I've seen what's on the disk. I'll have to tell someone."

"Rolly, you don't understand. If you tell people about this, the whole thing's going to fall apart. Those options you've got won't be worth the paper they're written on. There's only a month left until the IPO."

"Someone's going to find out someday, Fender. There were some men at the police station. They asked me questions about Anthony Kaydell. They already know something. They're just trying to nail it down. When they do, it will all be over."

"In a month we'll be rich."

"We'll be accessories to a crime, too. What am I supposed to do about that? Just take the money and forget I ever saw this? Hope the police don't figure it out?"

Fender's left hand went up to his forehead. He stroked his eyebrows furiously, looked down at the carpet. If this had been a movie, it would have been Rolly's chance to jump Fender, to leap up and knock the gun out of his hand. But it wasn't a movie. Rolly stayed in his seat. His leaping days were behind him. He had to be patient, wait this out, just like everything else in his life. He waited. Fender's fingers moved slower, settled in place. Fender spit out a sad little laugh.

"I'll bet you wish I was dead, don't you, Rolly?"

"What?"

"Just like you told me before. You wish I was dead."

"What are you talking about?"

"Right after the accident, when they were putting you in the ambulance. That's what you said to me."

"Fender, I don't know what you're talking about."

"You said, 'Why Matt? Why does a loser like you get to live?' Do you remember that, Rolly? You looked right at me and said, 'Why couldn't it have been you?'"

Rolly fell silent. He remembered nothing about that night. He knew the story he'd been told by his mother, by Max, but he still couldn't remember anything from the accident. He'd been driving. They'd all been drinking. Matt had been in the front seat, Fender in back. They spun off the road, went into a tree. Matt went through the front window. He was killed instantly. Fender walked away without a scratch.

And Rolly spent three weeks in the hospital, doped up on all sorts of painkillers and drugs. He wondered how many shitty things he'd said to people when he was drunk, oblivious. How many things would he like to take back now, rewind, erase? It was probably best he couldn't remember them all. He'd been a drunk for fifteen years. He'd been doped up and stoned and full of false ego built on a rickety structure of self-taught musical skills and self-pity.

"Fender, I don't remember saying that. I'm sorry. It wasn't just you. I was drunk, I was messed up because of the accident. I've said a lot of things in my life that I didn't mean."

"But it's still what you think, isn't it?"

"No."

"It's what you're thinking right now. That I'm some butt-licking loser who'd be better off dead. That's what you think, isn't it?"

"No, Fender. I don't."

"Well, I'm in charge now. With you, with Ricky. And King Gibson, too. When I have the Magic Key, I'll have something on all of you. Just like Curtis did. He told me I was a loser, too, but now he's dead."

"Where did you get that gun?"

"It's Curtis'. He kept it in a drawer in the bathroom, under a towel."

Rolly had a very bad feeling in the pit of his stomach, an unhappy feeling, a sadness that rumbled deep down inside him.

"You know something about it, don't you, Fender? You know what happened to Curtis."

"Who cares what happened to Curtis? No one liked him. No one will miss him. He was just some stupid little geek who liked to lord it over people because he thought he was so smart, because he could ruin everything for everyone by just clicking that button."

"You knew about this?" Rolly said, tilting his head ever so slightly towards the monitor screen.

"I was in the bathroom the night of the party. While I was there, Curtis brought King in, showed it to him. I cracked the door open, peeked in at them. He laughed at King and King left the room. Curtis came into the bathroom. He found me. He was upset. He accused me of spying on him, pulled the gun from the drawer. He took me back into the room, told me how the Magic Key worked, made me watch the whole thing. He laughed in my face. He said that now I knew everything, I was as guilty as anyone else."

"Who killed him, Fender? Who killed Curtis?"

"He killed himself."

"No he didn't."

"Yes he did. He killed himself. And I'll tell you how."

Rolly waited, stayed quiet. There was no sense interrupting. Fender had something he wanted to say. He had a gun, too.

"After Curtis showed me the Magic Key, he put it back in his pocket. We left and went back to the party. I was in shock. I couldn't think straight. I didn't know if what he had shown me was true or not. I didn't care. All I could think of was getting the Magic Key away from him, so he couldn't use it."

"What happened then?"

"The party broke up. Everyone left, except me. I hid in the closet in Curtis' room. In there." Fender sat down on the bed, waved the gun at the closet doors. "Curtis came in, took off his clothes, dropped them on the floor right in front of me. He went into the bathroom. It was my chance. I looked through his pants, found the key. I started to leave. I made it down the stairs and walked out to the patio."

"You put the key in my guitar case, didn't you?" Rolly said as it all became clear in his head.

"Curtis saw me. He yelled at me from up on the balcony. He had the gun. He told me to lie down on the ground until he came down. I lay down on my stomach. That's when I saw your guitar case, under the table. It was right in front of me. While Curtis was coming down the stairs, I opened it up, put the key inside it. I closed it up just before Curtis arrived. He accused me of stealing the key. I told him I didn't have it. I emptied my pockets, showed him that I didn't have it. But he started screaming. He said I was just another one of King's stooges. He jabbed the gun in my stomach. He called me a loser, said that Ricky always made jokes about me when I wasn't around. He said Ricky called me 'Fender Fuckup.' He demanded the key back. He was screaming, naked. I was scared."

Fender stopped, rubbed his eyebrows again. The gun had dropped to his side, but Rolly still wasn't going to try any heroics. Fender wasn't going to shoot him. Not right now, anyway. Fender continued.

"I kept telling Curtis I didn't have the key. He was screaming so loud. He was drunk. He was crazy. He threw the gun down and started hitting me. I pushed him away, but he kept coming at me. We fell into the pool. He hit me in the stomach. Hard. It hurt. I held him down in the water to try and keep him away. He was thrashing around like a madman. I held him down. I was only trying to keep him from hurting me, that's all."

"What happened then, Fender?"

"He stopped moving. His body went limp. But I didn't let go. And then I saw headlights. There was a car coming into the driveway. I got out of the pool. I grabbed the gun and ran back into the house."

This is the turnaround, Rolly realized. It takes me back to where I started this song.

"It was you," Fender said. "It was you coming back to pick up your guitar. I watched you the whole time. You saw the body. You ran away."

"So you knew I was here. And you knew I had the Magic Key. That's why you wanted Ricky to hire me."

"Yes."

Rolly sat, watching Fender, who stared at the floor. The song was almost complete. There were still a couple of notes missing, however, a couple of grace notes left to play.

"What about the body, Fender? How did it end up on the beach?"

"Walter did that. I saw him. He showed up right after you left."

Rolly remembered his close encounter with the Coupe DeVille as he drove out of The Farms after recovering his guitar.

"Why did Walter move the body?"

"I don't know. I saw him come in. He looked at the body a couple of minutes, then went back to his car. He came back with gloves on, waded into the pool, and picked Curtis up. He walked out to the deck and down to the lawn, and then he just threw Curtis over the cliff. I don't know why he did it."

"I think I know why."

"What do you mean?"

"Eyebitz.com had a life insurance policy on Curtis that paid ten million dollars. For some reason, Walter thought it was better if Curtis fell off a cliff, rather than drowning in the swimming pool."

It would have worked, too, if Rolly hadn't called 911 on his way home, if Bonnie hadn't stopped by the house that night to check on a report of a dead body in a swimming pool. A body that wasn't there. If she hadn't been called, she wouldn't have wondered about it, she wouldn't have stuck with the case. Perhaps then, Rolly could have tried to forget this whole thing, turned the key over to Fender. But he couldn't do that now. He had to lay down the overdubs, finish the track.

"When you brought me over to the office that first day, Ricky said he'd received an email from Curtis that morning, telling him the key had been lost."

"I sent the email. After Walter left, I sat here thinking about what I was going to do. I hatched a whole plan. I went upstairs to the computer and saw that Curtis still had his email program running. I emailed Ricky from Curtis' computer. I knew it would look like the email came from Curtis. I'm in big trouble, aren't I, Rolly?"

"Well, the insurance agents will want to talk to you. You might save them a lot of money."

"What about the police? They're going to say that I killed Curtis."

"Fender, the longer you drag this out, the worse it's going to get. You've got to come clean, turn yourself in. If you do that now it might not be that bad in the end. You didn't mean to kill Curtis."

Fender sat for a minute, the gun limp in his hand, still pointed at Rolly. There were little gears clicking inside Fender's head.

"You know what I think, Rolly? I think you're the one who's in trouble here."

"What makes you say that?"

"You're here tonight, aren't you, up in this room? You stole Walter's key and broke into the house. And you broke into our offices. You were here the night of the party. The Magic Key has your fingerprints all over it."

Rolly didn't like where the conversation was going. The acid rose in his stomach again. His sore, aching muscles tensed even more.

"Maybe you killed Curtis," Fender said, trying it out for size. "Maybe you killed him to get the key. You were going to sell it to our competitors. I know—you're an industrial spy, that's what this is all about."

"It won't work Fender. Someone will figure it out sooner or later."

"All you have to do is give me the key, Rolly. Give me the key and keep quiet. That's all I'm asking."

"The police will figure it out. They'll go over everything now with a fine-toothed comb. So will the insurance guys."

"No they won't. Not if they have their man already." Fender tapped the gun on his knee. Rolly didn't have much time left. He put his hand on the mouse and clicked the glowing "Do It" button on the screen. Curtis' message had been sent.

"No!" Fender screamed, turning his head and pulling the gun from his knee. Rolly dove from his seat towards the door. A bright bolt of flame leapt out from the gun, a huge crack of noise, followed instantly by the crash of glass and electronic circuits as the bullet smashed into the monitor screen. Sparks flew from the shattered encasement. The recoil knocked Fender off balance. He fell back off the corner of the bed. Rolly crawled out of the door, jumped to his feet, and ran down the stairs.

CHAPTER 37

▼

THE ESCAPE

Rolly ran out towards the pool, spotted a shadow moving across the patio, Fender, above, looking down from the balcony. Rolly ducked back under the door and ran down the hallway, turned into the living room, ran out through a large glass door onto the front deck, then down the stairs to the lawn. A cool wave of damp air rose up from the edge of the cliffs in front of him, a salt tingle inside of his nostrils. The incoming fog had covered the moon and much of the sky, making it hard to see anything.

He stopped, crouched on the lawn, hoping his eyes would adjust to the light. It was dangerous to go any farther. He turned his head back to look at the house. He heard Fender calling.

"Rolly, I'm sorry. That was an accident. I'm sorry. You scared me."

Rolly crouched lower, noticed how heavily his sides were heaving, how the speed of his heartbeat raced in his ears. He tried to slow his breathing, pull the air down into his diaphragm. A figure appeared in the living room doorway, the light from upstairs just enough to create a silhouette. Rolly flattened himself on the lawn. The dew on the grass soaked through his shirt. If he moved, Fender might see him, but flat on the ground he might not be visible. The light was behind Fender. It was darker out on the lawn.

"Rolly, why did you do that?" Fender stepped out of the doorway onto the lawn, slow, almost dainty. He held the gun in his right hand, stroking his forehead with his left. He moved forward two steps.

"Rolly?"

He was ten feet away now, turned away from where Rolly was hiding. Rolly held his breath, willing himself into absolute silence. His eyes had adjusted. He could see Fender more clearly. He had only seconds before Fender would see him as well.

Fender took another step out on the lawn. Rolly heaved himself forward, rolled over like a big beach ball, and rose to his feet just as Fender turned towards the noise. Rolly's shoulder came up under Fender's side, near his ribs, slid up to his armpit. Rolly kept moving, pushing forward as hard as he could. Fender's body gave way and they fell to the ground. Rolly landed on top of Fender with a grunt.

"No!" Fender screamed. "You can't!" Rolly reached up and grabbed Fender's right arm, pinning it to the ground. Fender struggled, but Rolly outweighed him by a good thirty pounds, kept him pinned. Soon there was no fight at all. Fender gave in. His body went limp. Rolly moved his left hand up along Fender's right wrist until he felt the revolver. He grabbed it out of Fender's hand, let go of Fender, sat back in the grass. Fender lay on his back, gasping for air.

"They'll take away my office. They'll fire me," Fender said.

"That's the least of your problems, right now."

"I'm going to jail, aren't I, Rolly?"

"I don't know. Probably."

Fender's gasping breaths turned to short little laughs. The laughs turned to sobs. Rolly heard a sound like a car door slamming, out on the street, or maybe in the driveway. They didn't have much time left to themselves.

"Fender, I'll try to help you. I'm your friend. It doesn't matter what I said to you after the accident. I can get you a lawyer, but you've got to tell me the story straight. What else do you know about Gibson?"

"Nothing. Nothing besides what's on that disk. He just showed up one day and met with Ricky. The next week he had his own office. Ricky told us he was a financial genius."

There was Ricky throwing that "g" word around.

"That's it?"

"I swear, that's all that I know. Until I saw that stuff Curtis put on the disk."

"How about Alesis?"

"She came a week after Gibson showed up."

"Anything else?"

"Like what?"

"Any kind of personal relationship between her and King?"

"Like sex? No. I didn't see anything. Somebody said she slept with Curtis."

"How about you?"

"No. We're only friends."

"How about that night that you and Alesis came to see me at the club? Whose idea was that?"

"King suggested it. We were just talking, you know, after you came to the office that day. I told him I was going to hear you at Patrick's and he suggested I ask her to come along."

"Did she know that I had the Magic Key?"

"I didn't tell anyone, not even her."

"Gibson called you at the club, didn't he?"

"Yes. He had my security card. Little Walter found it when he pulled Curtis' body out of the pool. He gave it to King."

"So King suspected you of stealing the Magic Key."

"Yes, he threatened me. That's when I told him you had it."

A distant doorbell rang from inside the house. Rolly looked back at the hulking mansion. He saw the quick beam of a flashlight flick through the windows, off the walls by the pool.

"Rolly. Rolly Waters," someone shouted. Bonnie had decoded his message. Fender sat up.

"Who's that?"

"It's a police detective, the woman you met this morning. I called her before I came out here."

"Rolly, I can't go to jail. I know what happens to people like me."

"What do you mean?" said Rolly, trying to play stupid.

"They'll kill me. Those guys there. They're criminals. They'll make me their slave. They'll rape me every day. They'll stick me with knives."

"You won't go to any jail like that."

"Yes, I will. I'm a loser. Just like you said. Just like my wife said. And Ricky. And Curtis."

"You're not a loser. You made a mistake."

"You said I was a loser, remember, a loser who'd be better off dead?"

"I was a loser when I said that. I was messed up."

"But that's what you think. That's what everyone thinks."

"Rolly, I know you're here!" Bonnie called. Fender stood up. Rolly held the gun up in front of him.

"Fender, don't move," Rolly said, then he yelled, "Bonnie, out here! In the front!"

"I'm not going to jail."

Rolly couldn't see Fender's eyes in the dark, couldn't see where Fender was looking. He hoped Bonnie would find them soon. He hated the feel of the gun in his hand. He knew he wouldn't use it. Fender moved to Rolly's right, away from the house towards the darkness.

"I'm not going to jail, Rolly. I'm not."

"Fender, stop moving." Rolly stepped towards him, but Fender was pulling away. One step, then two. Then out of sight. Rolly heard a terrible scream, like a soul descending to hell. He stepped forward, felt grass under his feet. Another step forward.. The grass turned to dirt at the edge of the cliff. He knelt down, reached to feel for the place where Fender had vanished, found nothing but air and the smell of the ocean.

CHAPTER 38

▼

THE CODA

It was early Monday morning at Patrick's Club, one-thirty a.m. The place was still crowded, considering there was a workday coming up. The band had just finished playing "Wrap It Up," the last song of the night. Rolly slipped his guitar into its stand and stepped down to the bar, got a club soda with two limes from Harry, went to sit with Moogus and Bruce on the back patio. They'd wait for the crowd to thin out before breaking down the equipment. If you went back in too early, there was always some drunk screaming at you to play one more, yelling for some stupid song like "Freebird" or "China Grove."

"Hey, wasn't that your girlfriend there in the back?" Moogus said.

"My girlfriend?" Rolly replied.

"Yeah, you know, the one from the video, Alexis or something like that?"

"I didn't see her. Where was she?"

"In back, at the table by the door. You can't mistake a well-tuned bongo like that."

"She's not my girlfriend."

"Well, if you're not talking to her, maybe I should."

Rolly stood up. Just knowing Moogus wanted to hit on Alesis was enough to get him up and moving.

"I thought so," said Moogus. "Still carrying a big hard-on for her."

Rolly walked into the club, stood in the back hallway where it was dark, looked out towards the door. Alesis was there, at the front window, sitting at one of the little round bar tables. She nursed a drink, something in a tall glass. There were a dozen customers or so still milling about, but she didn't seem to be with any of them. He stood there a minute, watching, half wishing she'd leave, but she didn't. He walked down the stairs and out towards her table. He paused to shake hands with a patron who greeted him, an enthusiastic young drunk who wanted to say something about the band, but seemed to have a hard time getting farther than, "That was fucking awesome, man," and improvising some air guitar moves.

Rolly nodded, separated himself from his admirer, walked up to Alesis' table. She smiled at him, a little sad smile, just like the one he'd fallen for last time. He wondered what she wanted now. He didn't have a Magic Key. She wasn't going to get rich and neither was he. The company known as Eyebitz.com was out of business, shut down.

The end had come swiftly. Curtis' email had gone out to the FBI, the Securities and Exchange Commission, the San Diego Police Department and Sheriff's Office, as well as the *Wall Street Journal* and the *San Diego Union-Tribune*. The local paper had jumped on it first, then the rest. Of course, Bonnie had been at the house to hear the whole story from Rolly. Like the good trooper she was, she tried to run the investigation according to the rules.

The IPO was suspended, King Gibson arrested and publicly revealed to be Anthony Kaydell. He was in jail now, waiting for the government to put together its case. If Kaydell had lasted one more month, through the IPO date, the statute of limitations would have run out on his earlier crimes. The whole investment in Eyebitz.com had been a desperate bid to spin his dwindling resources into new gold. A stockbroker the paper interviewed estimated Gibson would have received a forty-to-one payout on his investment had the IPO gone through as planned. But it hadn't.

Kaydell's arrest revived bitter memories among those he had swindled fifteen years ago; hope that they might get some of their money back. But Kaydell had nothing. Even the house, the BFH, was worth nothing. Kaydell had borrowed against it, under the name of G. Tesch. And now he was just a lonely old man, sitting in a federal jail cell, inspecting his fingernails, eating crummy jail food like the rest of the prisoners. There weren't any tournedos of beef on his menu.

Nothing stuck to Ricky. He got his get-out-of-jail-free card by claiming ignorance, told the authorities anything they wanted to hear about Gibson. It was Gibson, Kaydell, people wanted to nail. Ricky left town, went on a long surfing trip to Bali. He claimed to be researching new markets, making plans to have his motivational tapes translated into Korean and several forms of Chinese.

Alesis got to be famous for a couple of weeks. The papers and TV couldn't resist running her band's old publicity shot, as well as some blurry scenes from the video, usually when referring to Gibson's previous life as Anthony Kaydell, Ponzi schemer and pornographer. No charges were filed against her, either.

But that had been a couple of months ago. Rolly's life had returned to something approaching normal. He still played a couple of gigs a week, took on cases for parents or grandparents who hired him to help find their lost sons and daughters.

"Hi," Rolly said, flashing a smile at Alesis. He couldn't help himself. He wished he could learn to act more hardhearted.

"Surprised to see me?" Alesis said.

"I'd have to say yes."

"Why?"

"I don't know, just surprised. I guess I didn't think this was your kind of place, if you weren't on assignment, that is." Rolly looked away. He still found her attractive, found himself imagining forgiveness scenarios.

"I thought I'd come by to hear you play. I really was a musician once, you know. Not like you. I wasn't that good. But I had a real band."

"I know. I've got your record."

"You do?"

"I was at the swap meet a couple of weeks ago. I always look through the old records people are selling. And there it was."

"You couldn't resist."

"No, I guess not."

"What'd you think?"

"It wasn't bad." Rolly paused to consider. It wasn't a bad record, more mediocre really, like most of the records that ever got made.

"What are you up to these days?" he asked.

"Not much. I got a new job."

"Oh yeah, what's that?"

She pulled out a card, handed it to him. It said, "Executive Matchups."

"I'm working for a dating service. In La Jolla. It's very high class, for professionals."

"What kinds of professionals?"

"Executives, vice presidents. Corporate types who work a lot of hours. Guys who don't have time to get out and date."

"Rich guys?"

"Well, yes. A membership isn't cheap. We prescreen the women and men. They have to fill out an extensive form."

"Oh."

"I know what you're thinking. But this is legit. It's a real service."

"If you say so."

Alesis looked into her drink, stirred it around with the straw.

"You don't like me much, do you?"

"I don't know what I think."

"Because I wasn't completely honest with you?"

"I don't know anyone who's completely honest."

"That's a sad thing to say. Ask me something. I'll be completely honest this time."

"That's okay," Rolly paused.

"Go ahead. Shoot. Anything you want to ask."

"Okay," Rolly said. "That night, at my house, you moved my guitar case."

"Yeah. In the morning before I left. I was looking around for a pencil so I could write you a note."

"Completely honest, huh?"

"Completely honest. You have absolutely no writing utensils in that house, you know. You have almost nothing except for those guitars. I stubbed my toe on one of those damn things trying to find the bathroom in the middle of the night."

"You weren't trying to find the Magic Key?"

"No. Tony just asked me to make friends with you."

"Gibson?"

"Gibson, Kaydell, Tesch. Whatever his name is. I call him Tony."

"Do you always make friends with someone if Tony asks you to?"

"He's asked me for a lot of things. I listen to him, then I do what I want. It's always my decision."

"So Kaydell dumps you, fakes his own death while you're out touring Japan, and when he shows up again fifteen years later, you jump into bed with him, start working at Eyebitz.com?"

"I didn't jump into bed with him. Not this time. That was over. And he didn't ask me to work for him at Eyebitz.com."

"He didn't?"

"No. I made him give me a job."

"What?"

"I was having a drink at the Hyatt one night, six months ago. I was leaving the bathroom when I saw him get on the elevator. I knew it was him right away, even if he was older and bald. I watched the elevator, followed him up to his floor. You should have seen his face when he answered the door and saw me standing there."

"What happened?"

"I kicked him in the shins. He fell on his ass. I walked in, took a seat, and told him to make me a drink."

"Then what?"

"Oh, you know how cool he likes to play it. We talked. I told him I knew he was planning a scam. He told me about Eyebitz.com. I told him I'd blow his cover if he didn't find a way to cut me in on the action, get me a job. I read the paper. I knew how these Internet companies were making people rich. I read about a guy in the mail room one place who was worth two million dollars."

"So you blackmailed him?"

"He told me the statute of limitations had run out, which was a lie, I guess. But he knew I could make things pretty hot for him. There are still people in this town he owes a lot of money to. We made a business arrangement."

Rolly watched a bead of water run down the outside of his glass. He looked out the open window behind Alesis to the sidewalk. Two men were passing, giving Alesis the once over, then twice. Alesis pulled out a cigarette, caught herself, put it back in her purse.

"I meant what I said, you know, that night at your house."

"About what?"

"You are a nice guy. I don't know many nice guys."

Rolly smiled. "What about the other part?"

"You weren't bad at that either." She winked at him, a wink that meant nothing, but still gave him a buzz.

They were silent for a few moments. Gina chased the last of the patrons out of the club. She started counting the cover charge at her table by the door while Harry cleared the floor, set stools up on top of the bar. Moogus, Gordon, and Bruce had returned to the stage and were packing their gear.

"I'm sorry about Fender," Alesis said. "He was a friend of yours, wasn't he?"

"It's okay," Rolly said. He looked down into his soda, the clear bubbles clinging to the bright green rind of the limes. Had he and Fender been friends? Thirty years was a long time to know someone, but did it make that person your friend? If he thought you were friends and you never told him otherwise, did that mean you were friends? If he stuck around after you'd called him a loser, wished out loud he was dead, was he a friend? A friend was whoever was willing to be with you. A friend was someone you missed after he left. He couldn't say if he missed Fender or not.

"I was hoping *we* could be friends," Alesis said.

"I'm not sure I can afford you."

"You can't. Not if that's what you want."

"What do I want?"

"A woman to take care of you, bring you your slippers. Someone to slide under you whenever you're lonely."

"Is that what men want?"

"Every man I've ever known."

"You've known quite a few, I guess."

"And you? Is your record all tidy and clean?"

Rolly smiled at her again. She wasn't stupid. "I guess I'd say I've made some mistakes."

"I don't believe in mistakes."

"You're pretty sure of yourself, aren't you?"

"I do what I want to do."

"I'll give you that."

Alesis stood up, pulled her purse strap over her shoulder.

"Well, goodbye," she said.

"Goodbye."

Rolly watched her leave. It was a beautiful sight.

978-0-595-40267-0
0-595-40267-4